RESCUE!

HUMANITY FOUND BOOK 1

P. A. WILSON

FREE EBOOK

Claim your copy of Running the Game when you use the QR code below to sign up for my newsletter and cheer on Pen as she vies for a commission in the military.

1

J ocaster sat in the back of the room as befit his rank and standing. If he hadn't listened to Pen, and they hadn't been caught, they would be in the center of the room. But they were both under punishment for the antic. He reminded himself that this was a briefing, not a life sentence. If he was lucky they would get out of the room without making things worse.

"You'd think this would get more interesting," Pen said, reaching back to tighten the pins keeping her hair under control. "We'll be making rendezvous in three days, and we're still not planning a welcome party." She elbowed him. "You get special assignments; are you keeping secrets from me?"

Jocaster kept his eyes on the captain, sure that he would notice the inattention and apply another level of punishment to his hell. "Pretty sure there's no party. We don't have the excess supplies. Maybe later."

"You aren't bored?"

"I am, but if we mess up on one of the tiny details, *Zeus*

Rising might collide with us rather than connect. Then where will *Dark Prospect* be?"

"Our ship can take a few bumps," Pen said. She didn't sound convinced to Jocaster.

"Be quiet. I don't want to find myself in the brig for insubordination."

She sat straighter and the conversation ended.

Jocaster smiled. He'd met Pen when he was on an undercover operation and they'd been friends since. She was adventurous and spontaneous. Half the time he went along with her plans to make sure she didn't do something fatal. Everything about them was opposite. She was blond, fair skinned and blue eyed. He was dark skinned, green eyed, and bald by choice; his hair tended toward wild if he didn't shave it, and an officer with an afro the size of a small moon would send a different message than he wanted.

No matter what trouble they got in, the captain never seemed to take away the plum assignments. He knew the value of their partnership, even if it upset the order on *Dark Prospect*.

The daily list of outstanding tasks for the rendezvous was winding down. The captain moved to the front of the room as the duty officer covered her final bullet points.

When the captain stood alone at the front of the room, everyone shifted slightly in their seats. No one had been slouching, but they all came to a bit more attention.

"I know this was tedious," the captain said. "I'm here today to remind everyone of the purpose of our current mission."

He nodded to someone and a chart of the local area of space filled the wall behind him. Jocaster looked at all the blank darkness that crowded the edges of the image and encroached a lot farther into their position than he'd expected.

"This map contains our knowledge of the area, and what *Zeus Rising* has transferred to us. As we receive data from the remaining ships, many of the gaps will fill in. Until now, we've been satisfied to roam through space as individual communities. Now, we are joining together for a reason. In the last joint report from the ships close enough to send more than a short update, we learned that what started as a thirty-ship search for a new home away from the enemy has become a twelve-ship retreat from death. Our vessels are aging, and we need to find that new home."

The captain paused, but Jocaster knew there would be no questions.

"Sir," Pen said, raising her hand.

What trouble is she starting now?

The captain nodded at her. "Yes, Lieutenant Tromarin?"

Pen stood. "I think we all agree that this coming together is necessary," she said. "A question has been bugging me for a while and I can't figure out an answer."

"Ask away, Lieutenant." The captain smiled as he said it. Jocaster wondered if it was fondness or forbearance. Pen did have a reputation for keeping her cheekiness just this side of insubordination.

"When we find a planet, and I would love to be able to settle, don't get me wrong, but,"

"Spit it out, Lieutenant. We don't have time for the fluff."

A chuckle ran around the room.

"Yes, sir. The enemy has trouble finding us now that we're scattered, but they still do — find us, that is. Aren't we presenting an easier target by coming together, and an even easier one when we set up on a world?"

The captain nodded. "I'm sure you aren't the only one thinking that, but thank you for being bold enough to ask."

There it is again. Doesn't he know that he is encouraging her by doing that?

Pen sat.

"We know the dangers. But right now, if a ship is attacked, there is no one there to help. There is no haven for any survivors. No one uses the escape pods because there is no escape. Together, we hope to present a stronger resistance. Perhaps a deterrent. And by the time we find a home, we hope to have outrun the enemy — or at least have a long head start. Does anyone know the plan for what we do when we set down? It was our mission from the start."

Pen stood again. "The ship will be taken apart to provide for our needs on land. Shuttles can completely gut the ship in three days. The shell can be used for raw materials if we have time, but if not, it can be vaporized."

She sat.

"Teacher's pet," Jocaster muttered.

She smiled.

"We've agreed to alter the plan slightly." The captain nodded again, and another image replaced the stars. It was a list of components.

"When we find a suitable home, we will scavenge all the items except for some samples that we need to be present when we destroy the ships. To be safe, two volunteers for each ship will move them to a different area of space, blow the ships to leave enough trace for the enemy to believe we are all destroyed. The volunteers will return in shuttles; it will be a long journey, and potentially a fatal one."

Jocaster stood, and when the captain acknowledged him, he asked, "have we identified any planets that might support us?"

"Good question, Lieutenant."

The captain's approval removed Jocaster's fears that their last escapade had damaged his reputation beyond repair.

"We, the other captains and I, will begin that process in earnest as soon as we have combined our information."

Another hand went up. Julie Ackerman, junior Lieutenant. A good partner in the war games Jocaster played in addition to the training simulations. "Sir, may I ask a question?" The captain nodded. "Is there room for any survivors in case of an attack?"

The image behind the captain changed again. The twelve remaining ships and a number beside each.

"As you can see, some of our colleagues are in worse shape than *Dark Prospect*; the enemy is not the only threat out here. We have an inventory of the skills that have survived on each ship, and everyone can meet basic requirements. If we don't make changes to our mission, we will not live to see a new home."

JULIE WAS STILL STANDING. She clearly wanted more. Pen wasn't sure that the captain had even considered taking on survivors, but now that the subject was opened, she wondered, too. She didn't ask. Pen figured she'd embarrassed Jo enough for one session. The enemy had been chasing them for generations, and no one had ever lived to tell what they looked like. An attack was always a surprise, and always an obliteration. If the price for meeting new people was a boring reminder of what they lived with every day, then so be it.

"So, Junior Lieutenant, the answer is: we'll do what we need to. We hope never to face it, but there is room on *Dark Prospect* for as many as we need. It could mean short rations and tight quarters, but there are so few of us that we cannot refuse shelter. We need the genetic material, and if that's not enough for you, we will not hold onto our humanity if we leave our companions behind."

Pen noticed Julie clench her hands where they rested behind her back. Her face didn't reflect anything but respect; her body gave away the fact that she strongly disagreed. Pen wondered what she thought would happen if people needed help. Would she be happy to watch frozen corpses float by the screens?

The meeting was coming to a close. Pen leaned in to whisper to Jo, but her snappy retort was silenced as a cadet entered. The boy was in a hurry and didn't stand on protocol. He ran to the front of the room and interrupted the captain with a few whispered words. The captain stared at the boy and asked him to repeat the message. When the boy complied, the captain paled.

Pen's body tightened in preparation for whatever the message brought. She felt Jo come to attention beside her. The entire room went quiet, the small noises made by so many people in a confined space dropping away.

The captain sent the boy away and turned to address the officers. "*Zeus Rising* met the enemy on their way to us. Survivors fled in the escape pods. We have information that they made landfall on a nearby planet. We are going to rescue them. Return to your stations and wait for further orders." He marched from the room without waiting for any response.

Pen stood and fumbled for support. Everyone was suddenly talking. She needed to absorb the information. A rescue team? A planet? "We have to be part of this," she said, taking Jo's arm. "Imagine, landing on a planet. Not a holographic representation, a real planet."

He guided her to the wall where the eddying crowd was thinning. "And rescuing the crew and passengers of *Zeus Rising*," he reminded her. "This isn't a joyride. The mission is too important for us, for humanity, to let an inexperienced team go."

Pen grinned. "Yep, but everyone is inexperienced. No one has made landfall before. In the eight hundred years since we left earth, no one has gone more than a kilometer from the ship." She grabbed his arm tighter. "That means we are as useful as anyone." She was already planning how to worm her way into the meeting so she could volunteer.

"Pen," Jo said. "I don't think the captain thinks the same way. He'll assign it to more senior officers."

"You mean older, right?" She huffed. "We should go and tell him that it would be a mistake. Being younger is a good thing. We're more adaptable."

"I'm not walking up to the captain and telling him how to do his job. If we're lucky, we'll be included."

"So, just let them decide and maybe leave us out of it?"

"Yes, that's exactly what I mean." Jocaster looked directly into her eyes. "Don't get us into any more trouble."

Pen admitted that Jo was right to be worried. She knew he could lead a rescue team, and she knew there would be an opportunity to show the captain that Pen Tromarin wasn't someone who lived in Jo's shadow. "I promise," she said. "I won't do anything that might keep us away from the mission."

2

The wait for information was killing Jocaster. He paced outside his quarters, ignoring the communication beeps from Pen. Two hours had passed since the report. The only action from the ship was to announce a change in course. They were heading toward the last coordinates of *Zeus Rising*. No rescue team prepping, no call for volunteers. The captain, the senior officers, and the civilian leaders were secluded. All this time and the survivors were alone.

"Lieutenant Bryman, report to the captain's quarters."

Jo spun on his heels and ran. He was going to be on the rescue mission! Pen would be jealous. Of course, if he had an opportunity, he'd volunteer her. It wouldn't be the same on a mission alone.

There were two ensigns standing at the door to the captain's quarters. They snapped to attention as Jocaster approached.

"Go right in, sir," the one on the left said.

Jo nodded, pretending a nonchalance he didn't feel.

Inside, the captain and the civilian leader stood next to a

printout. The captain beckoned Jocaster over and pointed to the chart. "This is where the survivors were headed. We got another short transmission an hour ago. Most of the people got out."

Jocaster stared at the chart. The system was a binary with five planets. The survivors were headed for the fifth one. It was a long way from the two suns. "They should be able to survive," he said. "At that distance, the planet would be hospitable, if not long term habitable. What did they say when you told them rescue was on the way?"

The captain exchanged glances with the civilian leader. "Roger and I think it best we not communicate that."

"I don't think we've met," the civilian leader said, holding his hand out for shaking. "Roger Whitnal."

Jocaster shook the man's hand. "We did, actually," he said. "I attended a lecture you gave on settling new worlds. You were kind enough to answer a couple of questions."

Whitnal smiled, but Jo could tell he didn't remember. "I hope my answers were helpful. You are probably wondering why we decided to maintain silence."

Jocaster had been, but knew he needed to impress the man. "I assume there is a good reason. It doesn't matter, we're going to rescue them, right?" Was this what the captain wanted? For Jocaster to carry the news to the rest of the crew that they were not going for the survivors?

The captain cleared his throat. "We don't have time for politics, Roger. Lieutenant Bryman doesn't need to figure out what we're asking." He turned to Jocaster. "Lieutenant, we didn't respond because we fear that the enemy may have remained in the area. They could also have this information. The rescue party will be heavily armed, and we need a leader who will step outside regulations, if necessary."

Jocaster clasped his hands behind his back, images of

his last few escapades flashing through his mind. How much did the captain know about them?

"We want you to lead the team. We need you to pick who goes along. I'll make sure you get who you request," the captain said.

"You want me to lead them?" Jocaster needed to hear the words again. He'd meant what he said to Pen. He wasn't ready. He couldn't be responsible for that many lives.

"Yes," the captain said. "You have shown an ability to work through situations that others get mired in. Five years ago, you uncovered a scheme to cheat the officer qualification test. Since then I've kept my eye on you. I think you are the best choice."

"But there are more qualified candidates," Jocaster said.

"No, there are not," the captain replied. "Just older. Between you and Lieutenant Tromarin, you have plenty of experience working without oversight. She will join you, that's the only stipulation."

Pen will be no use in talking the captain out of this plan.

"I also have one request," Whitnal said. "I would like you to include Asher Jones in the crew."

"His qualifications?" Jocaster wasn't going to bring any spectators. He needed the room on the shuttle for survivors.

"Asher is combat trained. He is also well versed in conflict management."

"Excuse the question, sir," Jocaster said to the captain. "This isn't a negotiation, we're going in to bring the survivors back, right?" *Had he lied in the briefing?*

"You may find that the survivors need convincing, Lieutenant," Whitnal answered, ignoring Jocaster's clear expectation that the captain would speak. "I assure you he will not be a burden."

His mind was too busy trying to accept that he was the

right leader for the mission to argue about one team member. He had no room for passengers. He'd deal with his concerns directly with Jones. "How many shuttles? We need room for survivors — we don't know how many."

This time the captain answered. "You will have two of the landing shuttles. There's room for a four-person crew and fifty passengers — sixty if you need to push it. We think there are two hundred, possibly more on the planet. They landed somehow. You can use their shuttles. Worst case scenario, you make more than one trip back. The rest of the force will be ready to defend against an attack, if one comes."

The landing shuttles were supposed to take the entire complement of the starship to a new home planet. Two of them was a sacrifice. "Thank you, sir. I will choose the crew and be ready to go in three hours. Will we be close enough to the planet by then?"

"We'll be close enough for you to launch, but you will have a six-hour flight to the planet. The shuttles move faster than *Dark Prospect* in the short term. We will continue to move toward a rendezvous point as you complete your mission."

"If you will excuse me, I have preparations to make." Jocaster waited for the captain to dismiss him. "Mr. Whitnal, if you can have Asher Jones meet me in the armory in twenty minutes, I will be ready to assess him."

He marched through the door without waiting for the answer. Maybe Pen could help him believe he could do this.

3

He couldn't waste any time. Jocaster knew if he kept the mission crew small, there would be more room for survivors on the trip back. That might make a difference if anyone was hurt; maybe one less shuttle trip. It meant that everyone he chose needed to be able to do more than one thing. Handling themselves in a dangerous situation was a non-negotiable, but a few overlaps on skills like a medic, and a tech, and maybe a comm specialist would work. The more he thought, the longer the list of absolute needs got.

"Let me help," Pen said, looking over his shoulder.

Jocaster handed her the list. "Know anyone we should look at?"

She sighed. "Probably, but what about this Asher Jones guy? Is he just along for the ride?"

"Combat trained, or I would have refused," he said. Of course, the captain might have overridden him anyway. "Conflict management, not sure if that will be needed."

"You should get his file," she said. "And get him here ASAP. We know something about the others, but not him."

"I'm not an idiot," Jocaster said. "He'll be here in fifteen minutes. The captain put me in charge of the mission for a reason."

"Let's hope it wasn't because you're disposable," Pen said, jabbing his arm. "Seriously, if we have five people on the mission, we can split into groups. I mean us plus five."

"And you think you're the second in command?" Jocaster asked. He had no intention of letting anyone else into that position, but sometimes Pen needed to be less confident in her hold over him. It wouldn't help his future if the captain thought Pen took too much authority.

"Unless you can find someone better qualified," she said, joking.

"Like you'd let that happen." He punched a few icons on the pad and Jones' file appeared without any need for authorization. "He's a comm specialist, too," he said.

"Do we have time for him to learn the command codes?" Pen was flipping through files on her own pad, tilting it so Jocaster could read the screen. "Maybe it won't matter. We could have him as a backup."

"It looks like he'll backup more than that. The guy has creds in tech and strategy." *At least he won't be a burden.* Jocaster couldn't put aside his suspicions; Jones was added to the team for a reason, no matter how many skills he had.

Pen made a noise of agreement then tapped three files. "I nominate these. Ariel Moongazer, Liz Pernaz and Julie Ackerman." She flicked the files to him. "Medics, trackers, and techs. I have basic tracking and tech, so we have good coverage."

"Not enough coverage. We can do one more, I think," Jo said. "What about these: Raj Fraser, Lyal Wilson, Tula North?"

"I thought you said five including Asher? We only need four and you've listed six."

"No, you said that," Jocaster said. He laughed at the surprise on her face. "Oh, you thought I'd just say yes to your suggestions. Thanks for leaving me one space to fill. Yeah, I know you're right. We only need four and any of these will do. We can interview them and decide. I don't want to get stuck with someone who won't fit the team. We don't have any time to deal with conflict."

Pen laughed. "Okay. I guess being in charge means you should pick the team. And we have Asher, right? Maybe that's why he's been assigned — to deal with the team conflict."

"Maybe." Jocaster checked his schedule. "We'll give Jones a twenty-minute slot, and the others ten, one right after the other. I want to be on the way as soon as we are within shuttle range."

"We'll do it in the break room. I'll make the arrangements." Pen tapped in the orders and put the pad to sleep.

ASHER JONES ARRIVED on time for his interview. A few inches taller than Jocaster, just over six feet. Like most civilians, he was lanky; no one got enough rations to be overweight, and only the military arm bothered to keep up their weight training. He was blond, like about a third of the population, and he smiled a lot.

"Sorry that I was forced on you," he said before Jocaster could ask his first question. "I promise I will be an asset. Where we're going we don't need factions, right? Don't think of me as a civilian who is likely to screw up; think of me as if I am one of you. Can't promise I won't screw up, though."

Jocaster was sure the smile was meant to disarm him.

Even knowing that, he couldn't help relaxing his guard. "Your actions will determine if you are an asset."

Where did that pompous statement come from?

"I like that," Jones said. "No pretense. Okay, what do you need to know?"

The interview ended up being shorter than Jocaster expected. Jones answered every question posed, and he was fully capable of being a good team member. Surprisingly so, given that most of the civilians Jocaster knew were happy to leave the combat to the ones chosen for it.

"One last question," Pen said, finally joining the interview with more than note taking. "If everything you tell us is true, I wonder why you are a civilian. Being in the military has its benefits."

Jones leaned forward, placing his elbows on the desk; a very civilian move.

"I didn't consider it, to be honest," he said after a moment's thought. "All the rules and stiffness felt like they would be a prison. So, I took my chances and didn't enter the selection game."

"And how did you end up with all this experience?" Pen asked, looking down at her notes.

"Luck? I wasn't strong enough for the labor pool, so I got put in administration. It gave me a lot of scope for learning."

Jocaster looked at Pen. She made a note on her pad and nodded that she was done.

"Well, that seems to be the end of it," Jocaster said, standing. "We'll be mustering in the forward shuttle bay in two hours. Please keep your personal effects to a minimum; we need space for survivors. Your weapons will be supplied by the armory."

Jones shook his hand and left.

"Okay, either he's going to try taking over the leadership,

or he's lying about his skills and will be dead ten minutes into the mission." Pen closed the scratch pad and went to the door. "Let's see the others now."

Jocaster didn't stop her even though he craved a few minutes to digest the interview. Pen hadn't thought of all the possibilities. Maybe Jones was there to sabotage the mission on behalf of the civilians.

The next set of interviews comprised two topics. Military files covered the assessments of skills, and attitudes were also considered. These people were on the list because they had the drive based on their simulations results. Jocaster only needed to know if each of the candidates was willing, or simply following orders, and if any of them would be a problem on the mission.

When had Jo become so wishy washy?

Pen tried to think how to broach the subject, but everything sounded like a criticism and that wasn't what she meant.

"We can only pick four of them, Pen," he said. "Give me your notes." He held out his hand, fingers grabbing air.

Maybe it was just with other people, Pen thought. He had no problem bossing her around.

She opened the scratch pad and read through what she'd noted. "I didn't take verbatim notes, just impressions." She wasn't going to give him her pad. It was her way to stay in the conversation. This wasn't the Jo she knew, so she didn't know for sure how he'd react.

Jo reached for her pad again.

Pen held it close. "I think we might have a problem if we bring Liz Pernaz and Ariel Moongazer along," she said. Then, looking at the surprise on his face, she added, "I know

I nominated them, but I mean if we take both. Now that we know they are in a relationship, I'm worried that could put them in a position to decide between each other or the team, or the mission."

"We might have a problem clearing that hurdle; the pool of candidates is small. I think they'll be professional." Jo nodded for her to continue.

It was only speculation on her part, so Pen didn't argue. The interviews didn't matter to her. Jo had asked all the questions. She'd saved her fight for now, when they were making the final choices. If there was any opportunity she was going to put her mark on this mission, Jo wasn't going to get all the credit, or the blame. She was convinced that Jo was selected over her because their commanding officer didn't see Pen as a leader.

Her plan was underhanded, and although Jo would never hog the glory, it was time she started pushing her own career. The first way to do that was get her choices on the team.

"I'm saying it should be Raj Fraser, Julie Ackerman, Lyal Wilson, and Liz Pernaz," she said. "That combination gives us backup on the medic and tech sides. We won't need too many trackers because we have the locater, and I'm good at tracking."

"What about switching Wilson and Ackerman for Moongazer and North?" He looked at her and sighed. "Why not? What am I missing?"

Pen hoped Jo was the only person who could read her that well. She didn't like either of the choices. "Tula North is less experienced than Julie Ackerman."

"None of us are really experienced." He tossed his pad on the table. "You pointed that out. We got this assignment. You need to support me, Pen."

"I am," she said, suppressing the urge to say more. It was stupid to fight over this, but Jo seemed determined to push her into it. "But Ackerman has more time logged in tracking, and she's a medic."

Jo at least seemed to consider her words. "Ariel Moongazer is a solid tracker — probably the best we can get."

This was Pen's opportunity. If she agreed to Moongazer and something went wrong because of the relationship, then she could take credit for identifying it first. And it would be easier to get Jo to agree to Ackerman if she gave a little.

Pen realized she was wiping her hands on her uniform. It didn't help her feel less sleazy about the plan.

It could all backfire. Ackerman could screw up and Moongazer could be a hero. That thought didn't help either.

"Well?" Jo asked. "We don't have all day, and I know you have an opinion. It's not like you to hold back. I'm the leader, Pen, for better or worse. But I'm not planning on being the only decision maker. I can't. Despite what the captain said, I'm not qualified for this."

Swallowing her misgivings, Pen said, "Maybe Liz and Ariel will fight harder for each other and that will help. I'm still a bit wary, but as you say, you are the leader, so I'll back you."

He stared at her.

Pen wondered what was going through his mind. Then, he picked up the pad and gave her a nod. "Good. And you're right about North; she isn't ready. So, Ackerman it is."

She watched him send the request to the captain. His pad lit green beside the names after only a few seconds.

"We're good to go," Jo said. "See you in the shuttle bay in an hour. We need to do the pre-launch check."

They parted ways at the first junction in the corridor. Pen watched Jo walk away from her and wondered if their friendship would survive her machinations. She hoped that it wouldn't come to a choice between career and friendship.

JOCASTER STOOD in front of the small team. The shuttle was checked and ready to go. From the minute the shuttle doors closed, they would be on alert. Now was the only time he had to address them as a team. Pen was beside him, at attention and watching the other five members of the crew.

Try not to be pompous.

"This is our first opportunity to save our fellow travelers. The enemy made a mistake and we are going to exploit that. The people we are going to rescue survived an attack. They may have the one piece of information we need to win the war. If we can do that, humanity survives."

They straightened a little more, even Jones.

"It will be dangerous, and, if we are very lucky, it will be fast. The longer we must search, the more chance the enemy has to find us. You all know what will happen to us if they do."

No one showed fear, but Jocaster knew they felt it. His gut was twisting on itself with the thought of what could go wrong, but outwardly he had to be confident.

"This is your chance to ask questions, or air concerns. Once we board the shuttle, we work as a team, committed to the mission." He studied each of the faces in front of him. All were at attention and blank. "Don't pretend you have nothing to say," he added.

Pernaz flicked a glance at Moongazer and took a step closer. The movements seemed automatic to Jocaster. Pen might be right, but it was too late to change his mind over what might happen. The two women were as different as a black hole and an asteroid belt. Pernaz was dark haired, strongly built and close to his own six-foot. Moongazer was a redhead, although the curls were tightly contained in a bun. She looked like she topped out at barely five feet, and she was deceptively delicate. Jocaster had learned to his detriment that she was tough and strong.

"Speak up, Ensign Pernaz," Jocaster said. He hoped getting one person to speak would trigger the others.

"Not really a question, sir," she said. "Permission to speak frankly?"

Jocaster nodded.

"I wonder if this group is too small," Pernaz said. "If one of us goes down, we're in trouble."

"This is all we can spare," Jocaster said. "We... I picked this team for the range of skills you provide. Everything we need is covered twice or three times. If the captain sent more, then there would be fewer here to defend the ship. If...when we succeed, it won't be helpful to return to a destroyed ship."

She looked like she had more to say, then thought better of it. "Yes, sir."

"I notice we have a lot of medics," Raj Fraser said, his fair skin flushing. "Are we anticipating a lot of injured people?"

"Yes," Jocaster said. "Fleeing *Zeus Rising* would have been rough and I'm guessing people weren't prepared."

"How are we going to get them out if they're hurt? A patient takes up more room, and can't be crowded," Fraser asked.

"We'll deal with the situation we find, Ensign," Jocaster answered.

"Sir," Moongazer said. "If we can't find them?"

"I'm confident that we will," Jocaster said. Then,

knowing it was a weak answer, added, "Any decision about abandoning our mission is a long way out, and it's my decision, not a consensus."

Jocaster looked toward Junior Lieutenant Ackerman. Pen wanted her with them, but he'd seen her reactions to the questions; disappointment. He had to know why. "Ackerman?"

She took a breath. "Do we still have permission to be frank?"

"Yes, and you can all assume that stands unless we are in a crisis situation. I want your input; this is new territory for all of us."

"Why are we doing this, sir?" she asked the question staring at a point just past his shoulder. She was as tall as Jocaster, older than him despite the blond hair and ice-blue eyes that kept her looking like a teenager.

"Would you have us leave them to die?" Jones asked.

"I believe the question was directed at me, Mr. Jones. You don't understand protocol, but I hope you'll be a quick study." There was the pomposity again.

"Sorry," Jones said. "But I'd like to hear her answer, sir."

"You don't have to call me sir," Jocaster said. "Junior Lieutenant Ackerman, we are doing this because we can't simply let the enemy erode us to the point of extinction. Every human life is valuable to our original mission. We must find a way to beat the enemy, and then settle and rebuild."

"Yes, sir, but taking on more passengers than we can support is just as damaging," Ackerman said.

"A few hundred people will not strain our resources, Ackerman," Jocaster said. "You said you were willing to come on this mission. Has something changed?"

"No, sir." Ackerman stared forward again.

"May I ask a question?" Jones asked.

"You are part of this team, Mr. Jones," Jocaster said.

"I guess two questions. First, if I don't call you sir, what do I call you?"

This guy was going to be a smart ass, Jocaster could tell. "Lieutenant will be fine, or Lieutenant Bryman, since there are two full lieutenants here."

"Thank you. What happens if we feel your orders are putting us at risk unnecessarily? I ask for two reasons. As you say, we are all new to this, so you are not infallible. And Junior Lieutenant Ackerman here is not the only person who has a fundamental issue with the politics behind the mission."

Had he missed something? Only Ackerman had said something that would lead to that conclusion, and she would obey orders regardless. Was there some subtle body language that Jones saw? Were there politics from the civilian side that Jocaster didn't understand?

"We have trained for situations like this, Mr. Jones. Rescuing the survivors from *Zeus Rising* is not a debate, or a thought experiment. It will be dangerous, and it will be more dangerous if you challenge my orders."

"Just checking," Jones said. "I'm not planning a revolt, don't worry."

Jocaster bit back his response. Jones might be baiting him, or he might not. The man was skilled in conflict management, but that could just as easily be creating conflict rather than defusing it.

4

———

Pen couldn't wait any longer for Jo to deal with the conflict. She took a step forward and relaxed from attention. "I'm sure we are all focused on getting the survivors to safety." Turning to Jocaster she said, "We should get aboard. They are going to give us launch clearance soon, and we don't want to waste any time getting underway."

"Yes, perhaps this conversation would be better held in the shuttle. None of us needs this dissent on their file." Jocaster stepped back and waved the team inside the first shuttle, keeping Pen in the shuttle bay.

"What's going on with you?" she asked quietly enough that no one else would hear. "You can't let them air their grudges."

He sighed. "Pen, I know that. It's harder than you think to actually do what they taught us in leadership classes. Thanks for stepping in."

"Yeah, I get that. But they need to follow you. When the shit hits the fan, you can't simply ask people to act, you have to tell them."

Jo glanced into the shuttle, but it seemed that the others were checking out the control panel. "I didn't expect that they would do that. I thought Jones would keep his mouth shut until we needed his skills, if we ever did. And you are the one who thought Ackerman would be a good addition."

"Hey, I'm not the one who gave her a chance to undermine the mission."

Neither yelled, but Pen could feel one of their rare fights igniting. She paused to settle her mind and dampen her anger. "I'll talk to Ackerman. She doesn't have a record of insubordination; no matter what she thinks, she'll go with your orders."

"Too bad we can't just lose Jones," Jo said. "I guess we were lucky to get to choose the military personnel. I'll watch Jones. If he causes any problems, he'll find himself on shuttle guard duty."

Pen wasn't sure that would be a good move. If the civilian was a problem, they didn't want to leave him unwatched at their only means of escape. "We'll need to leave someone to guard him, if that happens."

"We can't afford to lose two people just because one is a pain," Jo said. He rubbed his face, a sure sign he was struggling to see a solution.

"You can't," Pen said. "You have to start thinking like a leader. If the captain assigned this to me, I would talk like one."

"Are you bailing on me?" Jo asked.

"No, I'm here for you," Pen said. If only he'd stop second guessing his choices, he'd be fine. She would never leave him to fail. The worst part about his flailing was that she knew the captain thought he was better than she was, that any discussion of how she'd lead the team was just a discussion. No matter what happened on the mission, she needed to do something to move out of Jo's shadow.

"Okay, well, I mean, I'll separate them," Jo said. "I'll take Ackerman in this shuttle, and you take Jones. On the planet we'll know more, and if we have to, we'll deal with them."

Pen raised an eyebrow.

"Yeah, yeah, it's going to take some time for me to get used to saying 'I'."

"Before they settle in, you need to tell them which shuttle to board."

The plan was to make sure that both shuttles had the full complement of skills with Pen flying one and Jo the other. If she took Jones, it meant taking Fraser and Moongazer. At least they wouldn't be bickering on the flight. "Let's get in there and finish the briefing fast. I don't want to be scrambling when the alarm goes."

Inside Jo's shuttle the team was arranged around the crew space, where the survivors would ride. A quiet conversation ended as Jo stepped into the space.

"We'll split into the two shuttles," Jo said with no preamble. "This one will lead. Lieutenant Tromarin will follow. We'll be using Alpha code to communicate our coordinates. If the survivors hear the transmission, they'll be able to understand it. If the enemy does, we hope it will slow them a little."

"Can we risk the enemy overhearing?" Julie asked.

"If you have a suggestion for how we communicate with each other and block the enemy, I'm happy to hear it." Jo looked around the group. "Look, the enemy is brutal and efficient. If they are on the planet, we'll be racing time to get to the survivors first. This is our only opportunity to save people. You all know what usually happens. Only debris, not even any bodies. We are at a huge disadvantage. The enemy might know everything about us, and all we know about them is that they are killers."

"Then I guess we want to learn about them, as well as save the *Zeus Rising* survivors," Asher said.

Pen watched Jones as he spoke. Was he a spy? Did he have different orders? Would he put the team at risk, or at more risk?

"Strap in and wait for the go signal," Jo said as Pen gathered her small group to leave.

AT LEAST THE simulations of flying a shuttle were realistic, Jocaster thought as he eased the joystick to sink the shuttle in to a low orbit. "Ensign Pernaz, scan the area for life signs. Ackerman, tell Lieutenant Tromarin to parallel our path and scan. If we find any signs, we'll put down in the closest safe landing spot."

Junior Lieutenant Ackerman transmitted the instructions and joined Ensign Pernaz at the readout for the scanner. The two worked well together and Jocaster's worries about Ackerman were fading. Everyone was entitled to believe what they believe as long as they followed orders. The code of conduct had very narrowly defined circumstances when orders could be refused. A difference of opinion was not on the list.

"There's some life below us," Moongazer said. "Animals most likely. I don't see any indication of shuttles or escape pods. I wish we had more information on the size of the vehicles. There's nothing large enough on the life signs readout to be survivors."

"If we don't find the shuttles?" Ackerman asked.

"We'll continue the scan until we have to return. If that

was you down there, you'd hope rescue was coming. I'm not abandoning them until we have no choice."

"Yes, sir."

The comm beeped. "Check the incoming," Jocaster said. Flying took all his resources, maybe someone should find a way to make shuttles a bit more automatic. When they had the survivors on board the ship, there might be resources for that kind of project.

Ackerman moved to the console. "Debris, maybe enough for a shuttle," she reported. "Tromarin is asking for permission to land and investigate."

"Still nothing on our scan," Moongazer said.

"Send the authorization," Jocaster said. "Tell her we'll look for another hour and join her. Maintain comm silence until we do."

In an hour they could check a big enough area around the coordinates that they might find the survivors. Now that they were here, Jocaster wasn't sure how he'd feel about all that open space with no solid bulkheads to keep them safe.

He plotted a spiral path around the location of the crash, keeping it tight so they wouldn't miss even the faintest indication. The survivors couldn't be too far from where they landed. Even with a ten-hour head start.

"There's something," Moongazer said. "Not enough for all the survivors, but definitely bigger than what we saw earlier."

"Don't count on it," Ackerman said. "Until we get down there, we have no idea how big the animals are. Remember the stories about things like elephants and whales that lived on Earth?"

"Let's hope we won't face large predators," Jocaster said.

"Well, larger than us, anyway," Moongazer said. "In fact,

if we're hoping, let's hope for only mouse-sized fauna and no enemies. A quick pick up and we go home."

"It can't be that quick," Ackerman said. "We'll have to wait until *Dark Prospect* gets here, and then make a few trips to bring everyone home."

At least she didn't take the opportunity to suggest they leave people behind, Jocaster thought.

"It will be a day," Jocaster reminded them. "Let's hope we don't run into carnivorous insects."

Their hour was up, with no success. "They could be underground, or there might be some interference that we don't recognize." Ackerman slid into the copilot seat as she spoke. "Maybe we should have asked Lieutenant Tromarin to make a report when she landed. Maybe there aren't survivors, just bodies."

"We'll know in a minute," Jocaster said. "Strap in, I've never done this before."

The two women laughed as they obeyed.

He just hoped he didn't crash alongside the debris.

"YOU WERE RIGHT," Kalin said. He waited for the translator to apply the coding to his message. The Adversary used the same language. The elders said it was because they stole the knowledge in the earliest of times. Now, he was glad, with the encoding, the Adversary would not understand his messages to Sola orbiting the planet, but he would understand their transmissions. It would make it much easier to track them and wipe out the ones that escaped the attack, and perhaps, take part in the attack on a new ship.

"Did you doubt me?" Sola asked.

It could be a pleasantry, but it could also be an accusation. If he could see her face, there would be no doubt. One did not question those who stood above, but they were not without humor. "Never."

He aimed his shuttle at the planet. It had been luck alone that put him in the exact position to see the rescuers land. He would never admit to benefiting from such an unsanctioned subject. To do otherwise would put him under scrutiny for a lack of belief.

"Keep your reports short, Kalin," Sola responded. "Track them. Your team is to destroy any survivors. The ones who came after are different. We need to question them first. We want at least one to interrogate, but if you can bring all of them you will be rewarded."

It would have been nice to know that before he'd laid traps. The survivors had hidden well. Kalin found nothing at the landing site to track them; no crushed greenery, no footprints. After dismantling the shuttles, he planted rings of traps at half a kilometer and one kilometer out from the landing. "It is my duty to obey," he said, ending the transmission. It would be dangerous for Sola to think he'd shown initiative by setting traps.

Both rescue shuttles were on the ground now. It was Kalin's first planet. Was that true of these others? He both feared and craved the day when the Adversary was gone, and they could find a home like this. His ship survived because they held to the true faith. The odds didn't feel favorable, but Kalin was a soldier and he would follow orders.

5

What looked like a crash from the sky turned out to be a systematic dismantling. Jocaster walked around the scattered pieces trying to pull any hint about the survivors from them. The ground was softer than the floor of a ship's corridor, so it would have absorbed some of the impact of a crash. The pieces were too close together for that, and they all looked cut, not torn.

The light didn't help. It was bright enough to show the details of the ship pieces but had a greenish hue that cast odd shadows. It wasn't from the giant ferns. The sun shone directly into the clearing. He wondered if the lighting on *Dark Prospect* was supposed to reflect that of old Earth or was simply a function of efficient lighting. Whatever the answer, this planet was disconcerting.

He rejoined the others. "Any ideas why they would do this?"

"Take apart their only way of leaving the planet?" Pen asked. "Maybe they don't know we're coming? Thinking they have to settle here?"

"They don't seem to have scavenged anything," Jocaster said. In his mind, he could almost see the various pieces fitting together like a puzzle. "We can ask the survivors when we find them."

"Perhaps it was to confuse anyone coming along behind," Ariel said. "If I was with them, I'd have done the same. Maybe come back when I've found a safe place to settle."

Julie stepped around a large piece of the outer skin of the shuttle. "These are pretty big escape pods. Maybe they had their hands full with their possessions and supplies." She picked up a bolt, sheared off at the base. "And who would they think was after them, if it wasn't rescue?"

"They wouldn't know if the planet was inhabited," Ariel said. "Or…"

"The enemy?" Raj finished her sentence.

"Are we going to stand here the whole day speculating?" Jones asked.

Jocaster checked his weapon to cover his annoyance with Jones. The man needed some lessons in protocol. That would have to come later; it was time to head out. "Okay, trackers, where do we go next?"

"One second," Jones said, annoying Jocaster again. "I think I know what this might be about. If you look carefully, you can see they haven't damaged anything. It looks like there are four escape pods here, in pieces. They did this so no one could use the pods against them. They knew they were being followed. They definitely knew we were coming." He walked toward the nearest cluster of parts. "Could these escape pods be reassembled and used to get survivors to the ship?"

Ensign Moongazer joined him. She touched the parts

and turned some over. "Yes, if you had a laser to seal them. And if you had the control module."

"Would a laser be part of the supplies?" Jones asked.

"Yes. Unless *Zeus Rising* has developed some new technology for cutting metal," Moongazer answered. "If they took the module and tools with them...it would be heavy but not impossible. You think they did this to help us?"

Jocaster set Pen to put the others to guard duty then joined Moongazer and Jones. "It won't help unless they left a clue for us to follow."

Moongazer stepped back and surveyed the clearing. She paced the edge and then returned. "They may have. I need to know what was moved and how."

He sent Moongazer to ask the others and called Jones to join him. "We moved these pieces. Let's put them back."

"If we can put these together, it's one trip back to *Dark Prospect*," Jones said. "Worth the time to reassemble."

Jocaster nodded and stepped back.

Moongazer was positioning the pieces of escape pod across the clearing. Jocaster hoped her idea was right, whatever it was. The faster they found the survivors the less he'd worry about being caught.

She stood back, nodded and then started walking back to him. Before she arrived, the comm unit flashed and Jocaster heard voices in his ear piece.

"*Vacat a molor. Zan parkal dunne makka leltel.*" The voice was harsh and sexless.

"Code?" Jones asked. "It felt like I should understand it, but... Whoever it was, I don't think they are on our side," Jones said.

"*Tosol Kor* my duty to obey." This voice was male, his words hard and cold.

"Translator got it," Jocaster said. "I guess we're not the only ones here."

"You don't think the survivors are using code?" Jones asked in a way that made it clear he didn't.

"Why would they use something we'd have to break? Someone followed them in. Or, maybe someone was here already?"

"Did the translator break the code and then translate the results into standard?"

Moongazer was almost to them. Jocaster wanted to tell everyone at the same time, so he kept his answer short. "Unless the enemy speaks standard, that's what happened."

"The survivors didn't do this," she announced. "If we are lucky, they did take the tools and comms, but someone else dismantled the pods. We might not be able to put these back together."

We're just wasting time.

"Where do we start out?" Jocaster asked, signaling the group to join him.

"No good signs, but if it was me, I'd be heading for cover, and the hills we saw on our descent are the best cover around."

The comm blinked again.

"Head toward the caves." This was a new voice. "Whatever happened, they were supposed to go for cover."

Jocaster looked at the faces around him. "Was that on the translator?" he asked.

"No," Asher answered. "Definitely straight standard. It seems we've found some of the survivors."

"We should head for the mountains," Jocaster said. "At least we can see where they are, and that's where the caves might be." He turned to look at the peaks. "Probably a half-day march if we move fast and don't encounter problems."

This is where our lack of experience is a problem.

There could be caves anywhere, but the mountains were a good landmark. The people on the comm might know more.

"Do we know where that communication came from?" Pen asked.

Liz shook her head. "Not for certain. We know they aren't at the mountain, and they aren't here. We need more to locate them."

Not helpful.

"What do we need?" Pen asked. "We didn't see any other landing place from up top. They clearly didn't crash here if they are looking for the people who did."

"There were a few landing options," Asher said. "One of them is about ten kilometers east of here."

"The river?" Julie asked. "Yeah, they could have landed on that wide bank and then hidden the pod in the trees. I'm guessing only one pod, otherwise there would be signs of others."

"I think we should try to find them, the people on the comm." Pen looked at him to see if he was going to argue. He nodded for her to continue. "Just two of us," she said. "I'll take Julie. She's a tracker."

Jocaster knew she was frustrated with his need to consider the consequences. He'd seen that look on her face before. But Julie wasn't the only choice. Ariel Moongazer was a better tracker. He'd like to send Raj because Pen was a good enough tracker, but he was assembling a small med kit in the shade of the wreck. He couldn't risk their best medic on only two people.

"Take Julie, make sure your weapons are working, check the charge on your comms," he said. "We're headed directly for the mountains. We'll leave some sign if we have to veer off, something subtle, so we don't tip off the enemy. You have three hours, then you need to catch up with us. I don't want to break off the rescue to come find you."

Pen checked weapons and comms and waited for Julie to do the same. "See you in a few," she said as she led Julie away from the crash site.

6

Twenty minutes later, Pen stood at the edge of the cliff looking for a way over or around. "We don't have time for this," she said to Julie.

"I'm sure the planet is upset at that," Julie replied.

Sarcasm truly isn't helpful.

"There's a path." Julie pointed to a thin line weaving down the face of the cliff. "Can you do it?"

"Yes," Pen said, trying to make her voice sound confident. She hoped the view was distorted by the perspective because some of the trail looked so narrow that they would be hugging the cliff to make any progress. Training sessions included climbing and spelunking, but a fall in the virtual world was not fatal.

"We should try to contact the other people before we go down," Julie said. She led the way to the start of the path. "If we can talk to them, we can get a location, save some time."

"And alert the enemy?" Pen took a cautious step onto the path. It was solid at least.

"They didn't react to the first transmission," Julie said, turning to face Pen.

Pen's stomach dropped. Julie didn't seem to notice how close they were to a fatal drop. "As far as we know." Taking a second glance at the trail, she said, "I'd hate to get to the bottom and find them at the top."

Julie shrugged. "Sure, just turn around."

Pen looked back, surprised at how far they'd come without her realizing it. The trail head was out of sight around the corner of the cliff. She put her hand on the wall of rock beside her and inched along, not looking at the edge of the path. She heard Julie chuckle behind her and gritted her teeth against a lash out.

It was only about ten steps to the top, but Pen couldn't get rid of the feeling she'd fall over the side. "What are you going to send?" she asked as they sat on the grass a couple of meters away from the sheer drop off.

"I don't think it makes sense to call them by their ship or identify ourselves that way. Do you think they know rescue is on its way?"

Pen hadn't thought to ask if the captain had managed to contact the survivors before they were out of range. "Let's work on the assumption they don't."

"We'll use their last transmission to identify them." Julie turned on the comm and waited for the green light to blink on. "Cave seekers, this is rescue one," she said.

No one replied.

Pen nodded for her to try again. "Are you on the right frequency?"

"I'll ride a few up and down just in case," she said. "Cave seekers, please reply. Rescue one ready to help."

She repeated the message four times before an answer came in.

"Never heard of rescue one," the voice from the first transmission came through.

"You were coming to meet us before you evacuated," Julie said.

"Where are you?"

Pen held up her hand before Julie could reply. "We don't want the enemy to find us first," she said.

"Reluctant to give out our position. The enemy is here," Julie said.

"How can we meet?"

"Good point," Julie answered. "Do you think this frequency is secure?"

"If it isn't we're too late."

Pen motioned for Julie to wait. She crawled to the edge of the cliff. Laying on her belly she scanned for landmarks. If the others landed where they thought and came back to see the shuttle crash site, they must be near. But they would be headed for the hills, and Jo's team might find them first. She pushed aside her irritation and peered into the distance.

The river was at the bottom of the cliff. It was narrow and curled around rocks that must have fallen. There was a point where the river twisted in a double curve before finding a way forward. If the other team had been here, they might have seen it. Pen tried not to think of the journey down if they had to go.

She crawled back to Julie and asked her to describe the point in the river where they could meet.

"We haven't seen the cliff," the voice came back.

"Why don't we meet at the crash site?" Julie asked the question without waiting for Pen's approval.

"We can be back there in forty."

"See you there," Julie said and then shut the comm down.

Pen couldn't believe Julie had given away the location. "If the enemy is listening, they know how to find the crash site."

"If they are listening, they'll find us anywhere we are," Julie said. "I thought you'd be thankful that you didn't have to face that trip down the side of the cliff."

WHILE THEY WAITED at the crash site for the others to return to meet them, Pen and Julie looked through the wreckage again. There was nothing to scavenge, and no matter how many times they looked, or turned over a piece of escape pod, there were no clues about the fate of the survivors. The only thing certain was that there were no bodies, and no blood.

"The enemy must have done this," Julie said. "Destroyed the escape pods so the survivors were trapped here."

"That's what we think happened."

Pen swung her weapon up as she spun to face the speaker. Ice-blue eyes stared back above his own weapon. Their landing must have been hard, as his face was swollen and starting to darken with bruises. His ancestry was as mixed as hers. Blond hair in spikes, blue eyes, and an olive complexion made him handsome even with the damage.

Pen lowered her weapon. "You're alone?"

"No. Just didn't see the point in risking all of us if it was a trap," he said. "Loke Ortiz." He pointed his weapon at the ground and whistled.

Two people stepped from the cover of the debris. The woman tapped the insignia on her shoulder. "Shanna Coalman. Good to see you, *Dark Prospect*."

The man stepped forward, hand out to shake. "Asad Miyamoto. You know where our people are?"

Pen introduced herself and Julie. "We were hoping you

had an idea. Are there more of you?" Three people didn't seem like much of a rescue team.

"We lost two people when we landed the shuttle," Loke said. "How many of you?"

Pen didn't want to stand around chatting. "The other five headed to the mountain. We should get going."

"You said shuttle," Julie said. "You weren't in escape pods?"

"We only got one shuttle out before the ship was destroyed," Asad said.

That would help, Pen thought. "Is it still operational?"

Loke shouldered his weapon. "Yeah. Why? You planning to take it?"

Pen shook her head. These people were so like her friends that she had to remember they were strangers, and they were brought up in a different way. "It will help to bring the others to *Dark Prospect*. Maybe a few less trips."

"We decide what happens to the shuttle," Loke said. "Our ship may be gone, but you can't just take what we have and make us like it."

She looked to Julie for a hint on how to respond. She just shrugged. Thinking that it was better to make their companions comfortable and let someone else deal with the details, Pen said, "Yes, your stuff is yours. We're just here to rescue you."

Loke grunted agreement — or dismissal. He turned to his companions and nodded toward the mountains. "We should go. I'm not sure it's healthy to hang out here. The enemy probably knows about the crash."

Jocaster stared at the stream running across their path. They'd been here for fifteen minutes; time enough to test the water and find it safe enough to drink, despite the yellow color. The mountains seemed just as distant as before. Progress was slow, and he could only hope the enemy was as hindered. At this pace, the trip might take days. But taking the shuttle closer would be a bigger risk. In the air there was no cover. And the survivors hadn't been on the planet long enough to reach the mountains if they went as slow.

"Should we go back?" Ariel asked. "They might be in trouble."

"I gave them three hours. And it's been just over two," he said. "We should keep moving."

Asher paced the clearing, his weapon down. Jocaster didn't like the man's behavior. He was supposed to be calm and controlled according to his file. Now he was like a trapped animal, looking for an escape route.

"Asher, we're heading out," Jocaster said. "Everyone up."

"There's something here," Asher said. "We're being watched, can't you feel it?"

Jocaster checked his senses, nothing. "No. Can anyone else? Raj? Ariel? Liz?"

"Yeah, I've got that itch," Raj said. "I thought it was just the strangeness, but now that you mention it..."

Jocaster raised his weapon and motioned for the others to do so. "Any idea where—" his words were cut off as a flock of what he could only think of as lizard-chickens burst through the giant ferns and tore through the clearing to settle in the water. They dove under the surface as one, and then took off again, running into the cover on the other side of the clearing.

Jocaster lowered his weapon and chuckled. "That was something," he said. "At least we know the planet isn't barren. You think they are edible?"

"Want to take a few back with us?" Raj asked, walking to where the animals had disappeared.

As he approached the first of the ferns, one of the chicken lizards darted out and spat at him, missing his skin but spraying on his boots. Raj yelled and ran to the water.

Jocaster saw steam rising as he stepped into the stream. "Are you okay?"

Raj swore and stepped back on the trail. "Acid. The buggers spit acid. Look at my boots."

Jocaster elbowed past Ariel and Asher who were staring at Raj. His boot toe was peppered with tiny holes. "Let's agree to give them a wide berth. And any other local beasts."

"So, I guess we got here just in time," Pen said.

Jocaster turned and saw her leading Julie and three strangers. "You found them."

"Yep," Pen said. She introduced her companions. "We should stop and put our information together."

"Not here," Raj said. "I'm not sticking around those things."

After the encounter, Jocaster wasn't sure any place would be safe. "We know what to look for," he said. "Ten minutes to brief, then we are back on the trail."

Raj didn't look happy, but he nodded and held his weapon ready.

"You want to report?" Jocaster asked Pen.

"Sure, I guess you don't have anything but a wild animal attack to share," she said. "Julie got through on the comm to Loke and his people. They landed a shuttle about where we expected. They agreed to join forces."

"The shuttle will come in handy," Jocaster said. "How many will it take?"

Loke glanced at Pen, who didn't respond. "Fifty. We were cut off, so it was only five of us. Two died."

"How many survivors can we expect?" Jocaster asked.

"Probably two hundred, maybe a few more," Shanna said. "Families, mostly. Civilians."

"So, they won't be able to help us if the enemy attacks?" Jocaster asked.

"Our civilians have training in combat," Loke said. "My family is in that number. I know they can take care of themselves. They have a few weapons, but they'll survive until we get there."

Jocaster could feel his defenses slamming down. This guy seemed to think his team was useless. That could mean trouble if they faced a fight. "That's good news," he said. "It means we'll likely get them to the shuttles alive. We have enough pilots to take all three."

"My shuttle is mine to deploy," Loke said. "She agreed that we didn't have to give up anything."

Jocaster looked at Pen. She shouldn't have made an

agreement without checking with him. "We should work together," he said. "Splitting the resources like that might be a problem."

"So, you gonna rescue us alone?" Loke asked, stepping closer.

"Gentlemen," Asher interrupted. "We should get going. I'm not sure when night comes here, but finding the survivors is the most important part of the job right?"

Loke didn't back down.

Jocaster knew he needed to save this situation right now or lose the leadership of the group. "We came here to rescue you and your families. If you don't want to cooperate, we will still do our job. Whatever happens, *Dark Prospect* is your only choice for survival."

"We could settle here," Loke said. "Being on our starship didn't help us. Why is yours different?"

"It's not," Asher said. "But this planet is not exactly hospitable. Raj just missed being killed by a small animal. I'm guessing the larger ones are more dangerous."

"I don't care," Loke said. "We make our own choices."

As much as he appreciated Asher trying to defuse the situation, Jocaster knew he had to make a decision. "Look, we can fight this out, but why don't we agree that we'll work together to find and rescue your people. Then you can all decide what to do."

"Fine," Loke said. He looked back at Shanna and Asad. "We'll work together. We can start by going in the right direction. The caves are to the west of here."

Ignoring the jab at his competence, Jocaster told Loke to take the lead and instructed Ariel to help him track.

· · ·

KALIN DIDN'T MOVE. He knew his suit would provide camouflage if he stepped back or moved to the side to relieve the cramp building in his calf, but he didn't want to take a chance. The Adversary might not notice, but if they did, he was alone. The rest of his team stayed with the ship while he followed the rescue team. What he overheard was more valuable than what he saw.

The planet was a good one. The shadows were deep. The green light didn't reflect as well as ship light, so it was simpler to hide. He brushed his shoulders to remove the film of pollen that had built up. There was no damage, but it was possible that over time it would damage the integrity of his suit.

It was the first time he'd seen these beings they called the Adversary. Kalin was not prepared for how much they looked like him. They had hair in different colors that didn't seem to be artificial. Everyone he knew had dark brown or black hair. The first time he'd seen the face of the one they called Loke, he'd been stunned. Did he have some defect, or was it normal among the Adversary to have blue eyes?

In the early days, some say even before the ship filled with believers and left their planet, their Holy Ones refined the flock. Everyone looked an individual, but all had dark hair and dark eyes. These people came in such variety; it was confusing.

He watched from the shade of a giant fern, safe in the knowledge that any curious animals would not be able to find him, as the suit took care of that, too. Another difference, the Adversary might as well be walking naked. Did they live in such a kind environment that survival suits weren't necessary?

The Adversary was getting ready to leave. Kalin would have a moment to report to Sola again. With luck, she would be in a receptive mood. He wanted her to ask for his advice, he wanted to say that no one would survive long on the planet and they should just leave. Or kill the rescue party and then leave. But she probably wouldn't ask.

Five minutes were gone before Kalin thought the Adversary were far enough ahead that it was safe enough to contact his superior. The communication signal was strong this time.

"They are now a little ahead of me," Kalin ended his report. "If I am to continue trailing them, I should move on."

"Direct the others to join you," Sola said. "You are to capture, not kill. The Holy Ones wish to interrogate the Adversary. It has been deemed time to eradicate them before we seek a new land to settle."

She wasn't going to ask his opinion. No surprise.

"And the ones who survive the attack?" It was dangerous to ask the question, but Kalin knew it was far more dangerous to guess at his orders.

"Let this small group lead you to them," Sola snapped with unusual emotion. "You can weaken them as you travel. We do not need to take all of them prisoner."

"I will obey," Kalin said. "I will leave two of my team to guard our ship. I will not fail you."

There was silence for a moment. Kalin held his breath, would he be reprimanded?

"That is acceptable. But do not get into the habit of offering your own ideas. The Holy Ones are infallible, you are not." Sola cut off the transmission.

Sweat trickled down the gaps between Kalin's survival suit and his skin. What had made him speak out of turn? This damned planet? Being so close to the Adversary? This was why the Holy Ones rarely sent flock out of the ship.

He dialed in the frequency for his next in command.

"We have orders. Riam, Lachi, and Imah link to my signal and join me. The rest will guard our ship."

Riam answered with the usual "I will obey." She didn't waste time with any offers of advice. A good flock member.

He didn't want to lose the rescue party, so Kalin slowly moved away from his hiding place. A feeling of dropping something and a slight bump made him look back. An animal that looked much like a broken egg lay on its back, staring at him. There had been no warning that the creature had been attached to him. He looked down at the suit that protected him — no marks or holes. Perhaps not all animals on this world were aggressive and deadly.

His signal would lead the other three members of his team toward his location, so no need to leave markers. Kalin stepped into the clearing and marched across to where his quarry disappeared. There was barely a heat signature, no broken fronds, no footprints. Whoever they were, these people knew how to track and how to prevent being tracked. They couldn't know about his technology. Why learn tracking when your suit could do it for you? He blinked to open the DNA tracer and followed the flickers of green and yellow that led away from the clearing.

8

The comm crackled again. Pen touched Jo's shoulder and signaled a stop.

"We should try to tune in to that channel," she said, hoping he would just let them do it and not push on now that he'd made the decision.

Jo nodded and asked Asher to home in on the static. "We'll stop for a bit."

"We've been walking for two minutes," Shanna said, turning to look at Loke. "We could have done this faster on our own."

"And, on your own, how would you take the people from the planet?" Julie asked. "For that matter, where would you take them?"

"Let's not get into that. We're together and we're going to complete the mission," Asher said from his position bent over the comm. He was switching frequencies slowly and delicately. "We're better off if we know what the enemy is up to."

"...*Holy ones...*"

"Got it," Asher said. "Just give me a second to lock in."

"It's the same voice," Pen said, relieved that the stop wasn't for nothing.

The itch between her shoulder blades eased at the knowledge the enemy wasn't near. The voice on the comm had a quality of distance. If the enemy was close, Asher wouldn't have to lock the signal in. She watched Jo and Loke as they gathered around the unit. There was still a tension there, but they weren't bickering right now.

The others leaned in to listen, each keeping one eye on their surroundings, wary of more attacks from the fauna.

"...*orders. Riam, Lachi, and Imah, link to my signal and join...*"

The static stopped only a few heartbeats later. Pen realized she had emptied her lungs with the tension. She inhaled and then said, "Four, at least four of them."

Suddenly the weapons that were at ease before were raised and aimed outward. It hadn't been a rational thought, but a sudden instinct of danger. Pen felt the tightening in her gut as survival instincts took over.

"It doesn't matter," Jo said. "Four or ten, we still keep looking for the survivors. We get them to the shuttles and take off."

"It will matter," Loke said. "We won't fit into the shuttles, even with ours — you know that. There will be more than one trip, and the people waiting on this planet will be at risk. And we don't know if there's an army or a few scouts down here with us."

Pen bit her lip to keep from agreeing with him. Or adding that the enemy ship must be close if they were able to transmit and receive messages in real time.

"We'll worry about that when we find the survivors," Jo said. "Let's get to these caves as fast as we can. Lead the way, Pen."

Pen hated the idea of leaving the details of their final escape to luck, because that's what it felt like they were doing. If they were alone, she'd try to talk it through with Jo, but they weren't, and she wasn't going to make him look bad in front of Loke and his crew.

"Just a question," Asher said as he packed the comm unit for travel. "Do you know why the enemy speaks Standard?" He was looking at Loke as he spoke.

"Why do you think we would know more than you about the enemy?" Loke's tone was casual, but he didn't meet Asher's eyes.

"They attacked you," Jo said. "It makes sense since you have had more contact." He took a step closer to Loke.

"You think we are spying for them," Asad said, moving to join Loke in facing off with Jo. "Just say it. You don't believe we're here on a rescue mission. You think we are working with the enemy."

Pen didn't know where that came from. Asher's question was reasonable and shouldn't have fired up their defenses. The crew and officers of *Zeus Rising* would have had some opportunity to study the enemy up close during the attack.

She watched as Shanna stepped up to Loke's exposed side. Pen lowered her weapon a little to reduce the likelihood of starting a fight. The tensions didn't calm at all. Jo was looking at Loke as though he was a spy. There was nothing subtle about it. The other members of her team were moving in to back him. Only Asher stayed where he was. Like Pen, he loosened his stance and observed.

"No," Pen said. "We don't think that. We haven't encountered the enemy before, so we are hoping you know more about them." Her words didn't calm them either.

"Why don't you want to answer?" Jo asked. "You can believe Pen. We're happy we found you. It will make the rescue easier. But we need all the information you have to make the rescue work, and to protect our ship when we get back."

Pen watched as Loke flicked a glance at Asad and Shanna. Were they checking to confirm their story? She hadn't been suspicious before, but now...

"We think they spied on us, and previous ships," Asad answered. "We think they use Standard as a weapon. Only when they want us to believe something, usually something that ends in a lot of death."

"We don't know for sure," Loke said. "It's worked that way. But not consistently. Sometimes it leads to a trap, sometimes not following the information leads to a trap. They attacked us for seven hours. It's hard to say what's true when all you have is seven hours of battle communications to go on."

"The simulations are chaotic," Pen said, before anyone could question the story. "Everything is so fast, you don't have time to think it through, just react."

"That's how it is in real life," Shanna said. "That's how we got separated from the rest of the survivors. There was no time to coordinate our positions. We were trapped in the forward section. The shuttles were there. We just climbed in and took off. We didn't know until we were clear of the wreckage that others had made it."

Loke cleared his throat. "We should get going."

I'M LOSING control of this. Jocaster watched as everyone, including Pen, turned to follow Loke. "Wait," he said, keeping his voice soft despite the urge to scream at them. "We can't just go ahead and rely on luck to keep the enemy from finding us."

Pen touched Loke's shoulder when he didn't turn back. He tensed then turned around.

"What should we do?" she asked.

At least that time she looked to him instead of Loke.

"We need to split up." Jocaster scanned the group. Having three more people meant they wouldn't risk as much by breaking into two teams. "Pen can take some of us to find any trace of the enemy. The rest will come with me to the caves."

"I'm not giving up on my shipmates, or my family," Loke said. Shanna and Asad stepped closer to him, again. Jocaster knew he had to find a way to stop them getting defensive every time he was about to make a decision.

"Let the enemy do what they want," Asad said. "We need to find the survivors and get off this planet."

"And if we get ambushed? Or attacked from behind?" Jocaster hefted his weapon. "These are only good if we know where to shoot. We're not abandoning anyone. It makes us more likely to succeed if we take some precautions."

Should I explain more? Jocaster wanted to be a good leader, and in the classes, he'd passed every challenge. In the classes, no one answered back, no one ignored his suggestions, and no one tried to take the leadership. Here, now, that seemed to happen every time.

Loke's stance relaxed and he indicated for Shanna and Asad to step back. "I agree. I'm just not splitting my group, we are too few, and those are our families, our friends."

Pen stepped between Loke and Jocaster, a little too late to break the tension. "I'll take Julie and Asher. We'll be able to move fast in a small group. Julie and I are great trackers."

Three in her party didn't seem like enough to Jocaster, but he couldn't put Pen's safety above the mission. Sending more people with her to make sure she was safe would leave the rescuers short. Plus, Pen would kill him for acting like he didn't think she could manage the task.

"Take Julie and Ariel," he said, knowing Asher's skills would be useful with his group. "Send a burst signal every thirty minutes to let us know you're safe. Only talk on the comms if you know the enemy won't hear."

"Okay," Pen said. She drew Julie and Ariel aside and started organizing them into a team.

He nodded to Loke to go ahead. "Don't get killed," he said.

When the team was out of sight, he walked over and handed Pen two grenades from his pack. "We have plenty."

"Let's hope I can give them back when we meet up," Pen said. "Good idea taking Asher. You'll need him to keep Loke in line."

She didn't wait for him to speak, just disappeared into the ferns around them.

He crossed the small clearing to catch up with his own team, feeling less shaky in his skills. If Pen saw that Loke was trying to take over, it wasn't paranoia or doubt in his own ability. An external challenge was easy compared to finding and fixing his own shortcomings.

9

Pen shivered. Now that they were stalking the enemy, she felt danger around her. It was immediate and deadly and not just fear. She couldn't tell if Ariel or Julie felt the same, but it didn't matter. The hair on the back of her neck stood up, there was an itch between her shoulder blades, and she constantly fought the urge to simply spray the surrounding area with fire just in case.

The wind had picked up in the last half hour and the ferns around them were in constant motion. A dry rustle coming from their fronds and the occasional click as a stem snapped kept Pen on full alert. On the ship, there were trees and ferns, but they were tame compared to the ones on the planet. No environment control here to manage the growth spurts. These giant ferns loomed over her and in places blocked the sun. Pen couldn't push away the thought that something was hidden in the fronds, something that wanted to eat her.

"It feels like we're being watched," Julie said.

"I thought it was just me," Ariel said.

Pen motioned for them to stop and gather in. Just

knowing the other two experienced the same thing eased her fears. "It's not just you. Is there any sign that we're not alone?"

Ariel pointed to the ground under a large fern. "Those tracks are everywhere. Small animal, or should I say animals. There's some evidence of those bird things, and another larger creature with claws as long as my finger, but a short leg. I think it's like the alligator in the vids, low to the ground, faster than it looks."

"There's no sign of the enemy," Julie interrupted Ariel, who looked to be getting ready to deliver a lecture on the local fauna.

"I don't know if that's good or not," Pen said. "We are looking for them, but they aren't the only danger."

"I think we should circle around." Ariel nodded toward a gap in the ferns. "There's no sign of anyone coming through here. I don't think the enemy would be stalking us from out this far. I wouldn't."

"Maybe we should be off the trail," Julie added. "The ferns might be just the cover we need."

"Going off the trail will be more dangerous," Pen said. "I don't mean we shouldn't do it, but we need to be even more alert. Are you ready for that?" Pen wasn't sure she was capable of ramping up her senses for long. If she was almost at her breaking point, what would the others be like?

"I have something for that," Julie said. "It's not exactly regulation."

Pen knew exactly what Julie meant. Xi was the illicit drug of choice for students who faced long hours for finals. Yes, they would be operating at double their normal level, but the crash was unpredictable and hard. Legal stims were the same drug as Xi, but in a lower concentration and even that had a hard crash.

"We can't risk hitting the wall at the wrong time," Pen said. She held out her hand for the package of pills, worried that Julie might start taking them against orders. "I'll hang onto them until we need to take the risk."

Julie grunted in agreement, or disgust at Pen's decision. She tossed the package to Pen.

"The best thing is to stick together," Ariel said. "That means we watch each other's backs as well as look for signs of the enemy. And we don't get our own tracks muddled with them."

Both Julie and Ariel were better trackers than Pen, so she agreed. "What kind of traces are we looking for? I mean there's the obvious — boot prints and blaster damage, but what about something subtle?"

"If we agree that life on this planet is still in the development stage," Ariel said. "There's just animals who live on instinct. No tools, no technology. So anything that looks unnatural would be an indication."

Unnatural? Everything about this place was weird to someone born and raised aboard a starship. "Regular lines?" she asked. "Cut branches?"

"Yeah, but I don't think the enemy is going to be that helpful," Julie said. "It's going to be a case of you'll know it when you see it."

Pen hoped Julie was right. The sooner she was back with the larger group the better. "Okay, Ariel, you lead. Julie, you take the rear. Stay close."

IT WAS EASIER WALKING between the giant ferns and tiny shrubs. Pen realized that the trail must have made her feel exposed — that everything was hiding from them. Now that she was covered by the fern canopy, she realized nothing was ready to leap out at them. The itch between her shoulder blades had eased, and she didn't feel like a weapon was aimed at her back.

Ariel and Julie called a change of direction periodically, saying it was to throw off anyone trailing them, and cover more ground. Now they were moving in the same direction as Jo's group but weaving back and forth across the trail. If the enemy was following, she was sure they would find evidence of it.

Ariel held up her hand. Pen came to a stop beside her, Julie joining them a moment later.

"Did you see something?" Pen asked.

Ariel pointed. Pen could see nothing in the shadow of the ferns. She took a step toward it and jerked back as Ariel grabbed her arm.

"No," she hissed. "Look from here."

Pen scanned the area. There was a pile of broken fronds blocking their way. It looked like dead-fall. There was a large fern just ahead of the pile.

"The fern shed branches," she said.

Julie pointed to the other side of the shadows. "Looks like there's a giant boulder blocking the way."

"So we would have gone into the shadow," Pen said.

"Yes," Ariel said. "The boulder looks authentic, and so do the fronds. I think the enemy gathered the fronds and took advantage of the boulder's placement."

"Tripwires?" Pen asked.

"Not that I can see," Ariel said.

"Nothing metallic on the scanner," Julie added.

Pen knew she should have checked her own scanner, but she'd fallen into the role of protector and let Julie and Ariel keep them on track when they stepped off the trail. Now that seemed like a very bad idea.

She crouched to get a better perspective, but nothing changed. "Let's look, then."

Julie stayed back while Ariel and Pen inched toward the pile of fronds. From their new position, the shadowy area received enough light that she could see the edge of a pit: it wasn't deep.

Signaling Ariel to stay put, Pen crept to the edge. Inside were sharp fragments from the crash site. If they had walked blindly into the trap, they would be laying there, bleeding, and waiting for the closest scavenger.

She pulled back from the trap and joined Ariel and Julie.

"So we know someone built that," she said. "I'm pretty sure it wasn't any of the creatures we've seen so far. I guess the enemy is close by."

"We should go after them," Ariel said. "Let Jocaster know, and then try to find the enemy."

"We are supposed to go back," Julie said.

Pen wasn't going to give up the chance to capture one of the enemy soldiers. "We'll tell Jocaster, and we'll track the enemy."

"But that's not what we agreed," Julie said.

"I know, but the enemy is between us and Jocaster's group. We can do both, right?" Pen watched Julie's expression as she processed the idea. Julie didn't like it, which was clear from the set of her mouth.

"Okay," Julie said, finally. "You're the team leader; any shit coming out of this is on you."

10

"We're close," Loke said. "We shouldn't stop."

Jocaster knew everyone was stretched too tight from two hours of creeping forward. He understood Loke's need to find his family, but if they showed up exhausted, there would be no rescue.

"I said we rest." Jocaster waved people to sit. "Ten minutes won't make a difference."

"Then we should keep going." Loke turned to Shanna and Asad. "You're okay to keep moving?"

Jocaster tightened his grip on his weapon. Everyone was pale and most of them had a tightness around the eyes that he worried might be the beginning of a breakdown.

Shanna rubbed her face and nodded. She was too tired to even speak.

"I don't care what they say," Jocaster said. "Look around you. If we don't stop, we'll lose our edge. Keeping alert to everything drains you."

"We can rest with our families. We don't need to head back right away," Loke said.

It took all of Jocaster's patience to not punch Loke in the

face. He wasn't a violent guy, but Loke questioned every decision and direction Jocaster gave. For the first time he was grateful for Asher's skills, even if it meant pretending to think Loke was helping.

"How do you know we're close?" he asked Loke.

"We're getting close to the caves. I know because we marked their position from orbit. I don't know for sure if we are getting close to the survivors." Loke kept his eyes on their surroundings. "For all I know, they are all dead or in an enemy prison."

His words reminded Jocaster that Loke wasn't on a rescue mission for survivors of an attack; he was on a mission to rescue his family and friends. Maybe that's why he was such a pain. Jocaster wondered for a second if he should hand over control to Loke. Then the captain's words came back to him. If he was supposed to use his skills of being unpredictable, he needed to be in charge. And he was right about conserving their energy. They had to start back as soon as they found the survivors. The enemy wouldn't stop looking for them or agree to a rest break before attacking.

"They will be in the caves," Jocaster said. "If the enemy took them or killed them, I don't think we'd be standing here. And the enemy would be gone."

"Is that supposed to make me feel better?" Loke asked. "My wife and kids must be okay because we're not dead?"

So much for empathy, Jocaster thought. "Maybe. But it won't help us find them. Or find the enemy. I can't make you feel better, Loke. I can keep us on mission. That means we need to get the survivors off this planet as fast as we can."

Loke deflated and Jocaster knew he'd won this round.

"Isn't Pen supposed to be checking in about now?" Loke asked.

Jocaster was happy for the change in subject. "She's about five minutes overdue. She's been late for every check-in so far. I'll worry about it when she's more than a half hour late and has missed a check-in altogether."

Rustling came from the cluster of ferns to their right. Jocaster raised his weapon and stood next to Loke. The rest of the team pivoted and prepared to fight.

"It's coming low," Asher muttered. "I just realized we don't know how tall the enemy is."

"Our size," Asad said. "I think we could take them if they were tiny enough for this."

The rustling came closer. Jocaster could hear the padding of multiple feet. "Don't kill unless they attack."

"Helmets closed," Loke said. "Who knows what defenses we'll face."

Jocaster closed his helmet, annoyed that he was obeying Loke and embarrassed that he hadn't thought of it.

A squeal hit his ears painfully before the suit muted it. He felt a thud just before the ferns shook from the impact. He held up his hand to stall any reaction from his team.

"It's not coming anymore," Shanna said.

"Stay here, I'm going to see what happened." Jocaster knew he should send someone in. As the leader he was supposed to survive to lead. His curiosity wouldn't let him wait for a report from someone else.

"I'm coming with you," Liz said.

He nodded and motioned for her to keep her helmet on. Whatever happened to the creatures, it was safer to stay fully suited until they knew the danger was over.

"Get down. We'll crawl under the ferns," he said.

Inching along on his belly was worse than he thought. The position left him feeling vulnerable. It would take vital seconds to get his weapon in position if they were attacked.

It was uncomfortable and slow, but they needed to be close to the terrain, and slow was better if there was a cliff hidden behind the screen of plants.

Liz tapped his leg, pointing to the right when he looked.

Jocaster crawled toward what she'd seen: a pile of rubble under a large fern.

He inched forward to peer over the top of it into a pit about half a meter deep.

It was one creature. Large, maybe two meters long, probably two or three hundred kilograms by the solid look of it. Ten legs on either side of its trunk explained the multiple footsteps. Its face just a round hole filled with teeth, like some kind of cannibal leech.

That wasn't the worst of it.

The creature was jerking, trying to pull its body off a spike of metal. Every move impaled it on another spike.

He stood, brushing the broken fronds from his suit and strode back to the path, Liz on his heels.

"Get Pen on the comms," he ordered as he joined his team. This time no one argued.

While Asher waited for a response, Jocaster reported. "Traps. The enemy has been here; there's a pit just off the path."

"Are they ahead of us?" Loke asked.

"I don't know, the ground was dry, so not a fresh trap," Liz answered. "We need to find more of them to figure out if they are moving in our direction. Maybe it was cut when they first got here. I'd probably drop some traps in a circle around the crash site if I was trying to stop a rescue or catch disoriented survivors."

"She's not answering," Asher said. "I'm not getting anything on any frequency."

Jocaster breathed slowly. Pen could take care of herself.

If comms were blocked she'd be on her way back. She had two expert trackers with her. They wouldn't fall into a trap.

"I don't like the idea that they are digging pits, but it's better than something more sophisticated with technology we don't understand," he said. "We keep going." The rest break would have to wait.

Even though the trap had been designed to catch someone off the path, Jocaster had his team fan out when they started. There was no sign of the survivors traveling the safe route, so he hoped their trail was in the ferns to the side. To call what they were using a safe route was a laugh; it was only a winding, clear thread of harder packed ground under the overlapping canopies of the ferns.

The team was broken up, Jocaster with Raj and Shanna, Loke with Asher, and Asad with Liz. The short-range comms worked enough to keep them updated as they progressed.

He walked beside Raj, both of them holding their weapons ready to fire. Shanna was a few steps to the right of Raj. The heavy canopy created a feeling of being buried alive, the lack of sightlines making him feel exposed. Neither would be acceptable aboard ship. On the planet it was just another pile of anxiety on top of the danger. How would they ever live land-side — if they survived that long?

"Trap," Shanna whispered. "To your left, five paces."

Jocaster turned and glanced where she pointed, suddenly feeling like that was the purpose, pulling his attention to a decoy trap while triggering a hidden one.

He saw fronds piled up, a bit too high to be natural since the ferns around them looked healthy. He scanned for trip-wires and motioned for Shanna to check it out.

She crept toward the pile, stopping just short of it. "Another pit," she said. "The edges are crumbling, so hard to avoid getting dragged in when it starts to go." She lay on her belly and lifted the edges of a frond. "Shit!" She recoiled and stepped back to join them.

"What?" Raj asked, so tense his weapon shook in his grip.

"Take a breath, Raj," Jocaster said. Glancing at the others he saw they all suffered from the stress of searching for the survivors and that feeling of being hunted.

"No spikes in this one. I think some kind of acid, or maybe it just reacts like that with the locals. There's maybe fifty of those things we saw before, the lizard things. Acid burns, some down to the bone."

"It's not going to be a pit every time," Jocaster said, trying not to visualize it. "We need to prepare for everything." He looked up at the canopy, a little sky showing through the dense leaflets. "It could be worse. Those could be hardwood. I can't see anyone making a weapon from a fern."

"They've had time to study the environment," Shanna said. "Those fronds were cut down, not dead-fall."

"How much farther?" Jocaster asked. "I'm assuming these caves aren't under this kind of cover."

"We're not making great time, five or six hours." Shanna checked her locater. "It won't get easier. There'll be rocks to toss on us when we get there."

Jocaster clicked on his helmet comm. "We should join up," he said into the mic. "Loke, Asad, home in on me."

"This isn't a great place to stop," Raj said.

"No place is going to be," Jocaster said. "At least here we know where the trap is."

He directed Shanna and Raj to search under the small fronds. If they were safe, they would be good sleeping spots.

Rustling of fronds to his right announced Loke and Asher's arrival.

"Down with the weapons. We don't want to save the enemy the trouble by shooting ourselves," Loke said.

"Probably should have a signal next time," Jocaster said.

His comm buzzed. "We're almost there," Liz announced. She stepped out of the ferns a moment later, Asad on her heels.

Loke scanned the area. "How long?"

"To rest?" Jocaster asked. "If we stop for a couple of hours, it should give us a chance to recharge."

"That's a couple more hours that my family is at risk. We can't keep resting. We have stims to help."

Shanna and Asad muttered something in agreement.

Jocaster paused. He wasn't going to be drawn into an argument, and he wasn't going to let Loke push them too far. "If you stop arguing, we'll actually get some rest. We need to let Pen catch us."

Loke looked ready to argue.

"Look, your families will be at risk forever if we don't get there. We've been on alert all day. The adrenaline is starting to have a negative effect even without stims." He noticed Asad's fingers twitching. "Look at him."

"I'm fine," Asad said. He clenched his fingers. "I'm fine enough."

"No," Jocaster said. "If we run into the enemy right now, we'll die. If we keep pushing, we'll arrive exhausted. Shanna said we have five or six hours to go. I'm guessing that will become ten hours soon enough with our current state. We rest, then we push a bit harder. We'll make up time."

Loke looked around at the small group, as if he hadn't noticed them before. Jocaster hoped he'd see the reality, not what he hoped. If Loke pushed, Jocaster might have to do something violent.

"Fine," Loke said, sighing. "Two hours. Two shifts, one hour each rest. Eat on your wake shift."

Jocaster assigned them to two teams. Loke would sleep while Jocaster was on watch.

"Next time, we take stims," Loke said. "No more resting."

"Stop wasting your rest time," Jocaster said. "Take a sleeping pill if you have to, and shut up." Stims might be needed, but the team was already twitchy with fear and fatigue. Stims would make that worse.

11

The traps weren't working. Kalin nudged Riam to get her attention. She was a good soldier, but sometimes she was too hyper-focused on a task.

"I must check in. Guard me."

"I obey."

He blinked open the comm channel and hailed Sola.

"You have them?" she asked.

That was the problem with command. They wanted periodic reports but always expected that he would complete the mission well before it was possible. It made good news into bad; and this time, he didn't have good news.

"No. They are cannier than we thought."

A long pause that Kalin knew better than to break. He imagined she was making an entry in the list of things he'd done to disappoint her.

"How close are you to the survivors?" The comms stripped any emotion from her voice, but Kalin thought he could hear the judgment.

"No way to tell," Kalin said. Another piece of bad news.

"There are no tracks. The terrain heals any sign of passage within an hour."

"Your sensors?"

Did she think him incompetent? "No life masses large enough. Our range is restricted by some damping effect. We're tracking the rescue team. They seem to know where to go."

"Following," Sola said with a sneer to her voice. "You have perfected that skill."

He wanted to tell her that he'd rather capture the rescue team. That he'd get the answers from them quickly and painfully. Her orders were the restraints, not his lack of bravery. But he didn't want a stint in the reconditioning cells. "Have our orders changed?"

"Winnow down this rescue team. Find the survivors. Kill only those you must." The link closed.

Kalin turned his attention back to the world around him. Riam was rubbing a fern frond between her gloved fingers. She was still vigilant to any threats, but the flora had caught the edges of her curiosity. Kalin watched as she stepped away from the fern she'd damaged toward a second plant.

"What is it?" Kalin asked.

She turned to him, slowly, not surprised by his return from the report. "Trying to figure out what happens to the damage," she said. "You were reporting for as long as morning prayer. Do we have new orders?"

"No."

Riam scowled. "We should not let them live. The teachings say the Adversary must be eliminated before we are to find peace."

"It is not our place to question the orders. The Holy Ones know the way to peace. We are only the instruments."

She turned away and pointed to the lowest frond to her right. "I broke this like I would have if we had passed by as soon as you started reporting. Look now."

Kalin leaned in to inspect the damage. He could see a bend in the axial spine. It wasn't broken. There was a thick film across where the break should be; it darkened as he watched.

"I think it will heal anything that doesn't break off, and probably will heal the wound of the broken piece," Riam said.

Kalin glanced at the ground, looking for fragments of the frond Riam had broken. They were not visible, but they were missing from the healing plant. At least the fronds they'd pulled to hide the traps wouldn't jump back to the fern trunk. "We've been looking for the wrong signs," he said.

"Yes, and now we can seek the barely healed marks, but it won't be of much value."

"Because it will take too long," Kalin finished her thought. "Well, at least we have information. Perhaps our prey has not yet noticed. Good work."

Riam nodded at the compliment. "Should I transmit to the others?"

He gave his permission and started moving toward the life signs ahead; they hadn't gained any distance in the time he'd been reporting. Winnowing their numbers was going to be difficult. There were two groups; any attack would have to take out everyone if the traps continued to be useless. Perhaps it would be better to attack closer to their destination — wherever that turned out to be.

"We will follow until we can determine where they intend to go. We will move ahead and trap them with the survivors if we must."

Riam grinned in response. He knew the feeling. Attacking and beating back the Adversary was more normal than this unsettling stalking and waiting.

ARIEL BENT over to check a deep shadow in their path. "Another one. How many of the enemy do you think are on the planet? We're finding a lot of traps."

Pen leaned over Ariel's shoulder. She wanted to give an answer, but there was nothing to hang a good guess on. "Maybe they know how to build traps fast," she said. "Maybe we're running into the only ones they built."

"If we could get the others on the comm, we could find out," Julie said. "What worries me is that the traps are in our path. If the enemy knows where we're going, they'll get to the survivors first."

Pen didn't think Julie looked all that worried about the idea of the survivors being slaughtered before they could be rescued. Was she still hoping to avoid bringing anyone back? "Without any evidence to change it, we keep doing our job."

"We did our job," Julie said. "We should join the Lieutenant, not keep looking for trouble on our own."

Pen bit back a response. If she'd known Julie would be so argumentative, she would have placed someone else on the team at the very beginning. But the woman was skilled and did follow orders that she clearly didn't like. "We're going in the same direction," she said. "We can speed up a little, just don't get careless. If we can see some tracks, or other evidence of the survivors, we'll be more help than just a few additional eyes on one track."

"We should be seeing traces showing that the rest of our team passed through," Ariel said. "I don't like that we have no comms and we can't find a trail. No one can be that good at moving through this thick vegetation without leaving a mark."

The itch that had been burrowing under Pen's shoulder blades intensified. Had the enemy taken her friends? "When was the last time we found them on the life scans?"

Julie's eyes flicked to her readout. "Fifteen minutes ago. We should be closing on them, but if we are, then something is interfering with our scans."

"And no other life signs? The survivors? The enemy?" Pen nodded for them to continue forward as she asked the questions.

"No, but we weren't expecting to find the survivors so soon. Maybe the enemy doesn't register on our scans." Julie hefted her weapon as she peered into the darkness to their right.

When Julie didn't warn her of danger, Pen stepped forward. Her muscles were burning from the tension of every step. Perhaps it hadn't occurred to the enemy to set tripwires, but they couldn't risk it. "Maybe we'll get some intelligence on the enemy. Something the captain can use when we get back to the ship," she said.

"Let's hope we get more than that," Ariel said. "A bunch of new recruits and some information would be perfect."

"Recruits?" Pen wondered what the survivors faced on *Dark Prospect* when they returned. They wouldn't survive The Game, so unlikely they'd be in the officer ranks, unless the captain made exceptions for survivors who'd been in command. Would they be forced into the combat troops? Her thoughts were interrupted by the sight of a sliver of metal at the edge of the shadows to her right. "Ariel, check that out."

The tracker pivoted and stepped to the metal. She

checked the ground around it before delicately picking it up. "Meal wrapper," she announced. "Not one of ours, but it's similar. Probably one of Loke's people."

"Could it be from the survivors?" Pen asked.

Ariel glanced at the ground again and then held out the metal for Pen and Julie to inspect. "I don't think it's been here long enough for that. Look at the edges; there's some green. I think the ground was already starting to cover it. But I can smell the residue of the meal, so it can't have been there long."

"It means we're close," Julie said. "We should move faster and catch up."

"We can't risk speed," Pen said.

"We aren't finding anything useful out here," Julie snapped. "We should catch up and let Jocaster decide. We've done what he ordered."

Pen considered an argument, but realized she had nothing to say. Julie was right; there was nothing out here to be found. No tracks, nothing but traps they could avoid now that they knew about them. She'd find a way to get Jo to send them on another mission. She was missing him anyway, and they needed to figure out the problem with the comms before splitting the team again.

"Single file," she said. "Ariel, lead the way. Set a pace that won't get us killed."

12

I t was coming up on time for another rest. Jocaster knew Loke would hate it, but they needed to stay on full alert all the time and that meant rest breaks. And it meant another opportunity for Asher to try getting Pen on the comms again. His gut burned with worry about her. Even without the comms, Pen's team should have caught up. There were too many ways for her to die on this planet. Not just the enemy, but the animals and natural hazards they never had to worry about aboard ship.

"Stop," Loke whispered.

Jocaster froze, watching as the man knelt in front of a stack of fronds. Now that they knew what to look for, these screamed fake. The ferns they'd passed so far didn't shed piles of fronds.

Loke looked up and beckoned Jocaster over. "Look at this," he said, pointing to the ends of the closest branch. "Wet. This trap is new."

The enemy was nearby. Jocaster felt his stomach tighten with fear. Were they being watched? There was no sound of anyone coming from the shadows, but that didn't mean anything. The enemy could be camouflaged so well that they could be standing right in front of them. The only assurance he could find that they weren't was that he still stood. From what little they knew of the enemy, they didn't hide in the shadows, they attacked.

It added to his worry about Pen and her team. Were they captured? He hoped that Pen and her team were still free. Before he could decide to turn back to find Pen, he watched as the cut end of the frond began to seal off. "What the hell?" He reached for another branch.

Loke slapped his arm away. "Don't be an idiot. You could trigger the trap. Just because they hide it the same way doesn't mean it's the same danger."

Jocaster pointed to the cut ends around them. All were healing as they watched. "We have no idea how close the enemy has been, or the survivors. I guess it explains why the trail is cold."

Loke reached to pull him back. "We're still headed for the caves. My family can't be too far ahead of us. But maybe they are ahead of the traps, making better time."

For the first time Jocaster agreed with Loke. They needed speed. He wanted Pen to rejoin them with Julie and Ariel, but they couldn't delay. Loke didn't see it, but Jocaster wasn't going to lose his team to fatigue. They would move faster with a rest break. "We'll stop for fifteen," he said. Then he glanced at the trap again. "And we'll test this healing thing. Cut a frond off a fern and let's time it."

"So, we take stims and keep going?" Loke patted his medical pouch.

"No. We'll try getting Pen's team on the comms. We'll see how much head start the enemy has by how long it takes to heal the cut while we take fifteen to rest. We'll move faster after that."

"My family, my friends," Loke said.

"Like you said, they're ahead of the enemy. The fact that the traps are fresh means the enemy is with us, not them. Maybe they don't know where the survivors are," Jocaster said. "Maybe we can use that to our advantage. Set a trap or two of our own."

"And if you're wrong?" Loke glanced over his shoulder at the rest of his team.

Jocaster followed his gaze. They were all jumpy, but Asad and Shanna were twitching. "You told your team to take stims," he said.

"Just one," Loke said. "They'll be fine."

Jocaster looked at Loke again. There was a twitch at the corner of his mouth. "And you?"

"I'll do what it takes."

If their positions were reversed, Jocaster couldn't guarantee that he would refrain from stims. The problem was that his team needed rest and Loke's wouldn't be able to. "Cut a fern. I'll send Shanna ahead to scout and Asad to the rear. You stay with me, and don't do this again."

"Just get your people to take a stim and we can keep moving."

"And if we'd all been strung out, we would have missed this information." Jocaster pointed to the cut frond which was fully healed. "This might make the difference. Don't make decisions without me."

"I lead my team."

"It's all my team," Jocaster said. "You need us, we need you. Even if I wanted to work on stims now, we can't because your people need to come down first. When did you take them?"

Loke's eyes blazed with anger. Another issue with stims: rage. Then the emotion suddenly deflated. "We'll be back to normal in about an hour."

"Then we'll stop again in an hour." If they hadn't heard from Pen by then, he was sending people to find them. Stims would be helpful for that mission.

PEN STARED at the tracking screen. She'd taken it from Julie because she didn't want to sound like a pest asking for updates every few minutes. It didn't end her need to know if there were any signs of Jocaster's group, the survivors, or the enemy, it just let her check quietly.

The screen flickered. It went too fast to tell how many life signs showed, but it was less than she expected of the survivors, who were probably still too far away, so it could be Jocaster's team. Or the enemy. She refused to worry about it. The fact that they had some information was better than none.

"We must be coming into range," she said. "I don't know how they could have gotten so far ahead."

"Pen, there's no way they could travel that fast," Ariel said. "Even if they aren't looking out for traps, they won't have a clear enough path to run. And the comms still don't work, so it's something from the enemy, or the planet."

"You think the planet is interfering with our equipment?" Pen looked around.

"This place is weird. Who knows what it's capable of," Ariel said. "I feel like it's watching us and setting its own traps. Ones we can't avoid."

"Don't be an idiot," Julie said. "It's just a planet. We should close the distance. We haven't seen a trap for at least an hour. It must be safe to speed up."

Julie never gave up her push to hurry back to Jocaster. Pen let the locater hang by its strap and joined the two women who were discussing the choice of going left or right around a fern that filled their path as far as Pen could see. "What about going through?"

Ariel pushed a finger between two fronds and peeked inside. "We've been trying not to leave a trail. Basic tracker technique. But I should have thought of that. The enemy is ahead of us based on the traps. So, we don't need to worry about them tracking us."

"Let's go then." Julie took a step forward.

Pen grabbed her arm. "We don't know what it's like in there. Don't just march in, you know better than that."

Julie shook off her hand. "I know. I was going to check it out and then let you know." The words came out as a huff.

Pen knew it wasn't the time to deal with the insubordination, but Julie needed to know that Pen wouldn't take the attitude for long. "I decide who goes first."

Julie glared at her for a fraction of a second, then she looked away and agreed.

"This is different from looking for traps," Pen said. "Ariel is our best tracker, not just the best on our team, but probably the best on the ship. That means she's way better than you or I."

"I'm happy to go first," Ariel said.

"I know," Pen said. "Just be careful, and put on your mask. We don't know what's in the air inside. Even from here, I can feel the temperature change. This is the biggest fern tree we've seen, so don't assume anything."

Ariel slid her helmet closed, checked her weapon, and zipped her coverall. She tapped the side of her helmet. "Is the local link working?"

Pen pulled her own helmet closed and answered, "Is it?"

Ariel nodded. She pushed a gloved hand through the curtain of fronds and slipped through the gap. When she passed there was no evidence of it.

"It's darker in here too," Ariel said.

"Any problems?" Julie asked over the comms.

Pen glanced over at her. Julie was ready to follow Ariel. Pen held up a hand to make sure she knew that they would wait for Ariel to give them the green light.

"My helmet says there's more dioxide, but it's breathable. Let's not take the chance," she said. "Come on through with your helmets on."

Pen motioned for Julie to precede her. When she joined them, Pen felt like she'd moved to a different planet. The air might be breathable, but it was green. The light was barely enough to let her see her way.

Ariel pointed across the dome of fronds. "I think it's a path."

Directly across from them, the fronds of this tree met the fronds of another and overlapped, leaving a space into the next canopy. "Is it going in the right direction?"

"Yes," Ariel said. "Maybe Jocaster and the rest found something like this. It would explain how they got farther ahead than we expected."

The feeling of being stalked was gone. Pen wasn't exactly comfortable, but it felt more like the corridors of the ship than the open planet. "Okay, let's try going as long as it's pointing where we want."

"There are footprints," Julie said, nodding to the right of their position. "Big ones."

Ariel pointed to the left. "There are more over there. The prints aren't distinct enough to tell if they are animals or human, or the enemy if we knew what their prints looked like. Just keep your eyes open and we should be fine."

Pen looked ahead. The prints didn't pass through the space, just clustered in groups as though this were a meeting place. "Let's go. Julie take up the rear. Ariel set the path."

As Pen followed Ariel through the series of fern tree canopies, she imagined what it looked like from outside, like a series of Venn diagrams. She chuckled. They were making good time and the flickers of life signs came more frequently and stayed on-screen longer. Now she was confident that they were closing in on Jocaster.

"Stop," Ariel's voice on the comm was urgent.

"Trap?" Pen asked. The path didn't veer so it wasn't a direction change.

"One," Ariel gestured into the gloom at the edge of the opening. "It's different and might be natural."

Pen squinted. Filaments waved in a breeze she couldn't feel. "Julie, check it out."

Julie checked her suit again before stepping toward the trap. Pen watched as she walked the length of the opening. "It's right across our path," Julie said. "It seems to be coming from the ferns."

"I don't like this," Pen said. "Come back and we'll find a way around."

Julie didn't respond. Pen watched as she waved her arm through the filaments and stepped back. She looked at her arm and brushed something off. "No acid. It breaks easily. We can go through."

"I said to come back." Pen let her anger flow through the words. Julie's actions could have killed them if it had turned out to be a defense for the ferns. As soon as they had privacy, Julie was getting that reprimand. "Get back here now."

"Fine," Julie said. She marched to join Pen and Ariel. "Do you see another way?"

Pen wasn't going to pass up the opportunity to keep moving, but that didn't mean Julie could get away with her attitude. She wasn't going to embarrass Ariel by dressing Julie down in front of her, but if Julie was determined to take risks, Pen could take advantage of it. "You go first. Remember, your job is to find a safe way through, not just a fast way."

Behind the faceplate, Julie grinned. "Yes, ma'am."

"Ariel, take the rear," Pen said.

They approached the curtain of filaments. It was thicker now, like the plant was generating a stronger barrier after Julie's action. Julie passed through, brushing stray threads. Pen heard the whisper of the strands as they slid around her suit. She shook off the ones that clung to her.

"Help!" Ariel's voice cut through Pen's helmet.

She turned. Ariel was fighting to break free of the filaments, which had thickened to ropes. They were curling around her like snakes and pulling her down into the soft ground.

"Julie!" Pen ran toward Ariel, setting her weapon to low charge. She fired at Ariel. Her suit would protect her, but maybe the shot could burn the ropes away. No luck.

"Go back," Ariel said. "Don't get trapped. I'm not getting free."

"Julie, cut them off," Pen ordered. "We can't just let them have her."

Julie tugged Pen away. "She's right. Her suit is giving way."

As Pen watched, Ariel's helmet cracked under the pressure of a rope curling around it. Then Ariel gasped and choked. One of the strands wrapped around her neck. Pen heard a snap and then Ariel stopped fighting.

"No," Pen whispered. How could that have happened so quickly? She took a step forward and then stopped as a rope reached for her.

"Pen, we have to go," Julie yelled. "We have to find a way out of here and get back on the path."

13

A riel was gone.

Pen's training told her what to do, but it didn't help her with the emotions that tore through her. It was her fault. She should have made them come out of cover, or she should have spent less time deciding what to do. If they'd just gone through, the fern wouldn't have had time to create the ropes. They wouldn't know it was possible, but at least Ariel would be alive.

And the shameful emotion that flooded her: relief. It could have been her. If she'd taken the rear, she would be a dead body right now.

"Pen," Julie said, dragging her back to the real world.

"I know we need to go faster," Pen said. They stood outside the canopied fern path. Somehow the enemy had known not to go inside, or perhaps they'd lost one of theirs, or maybe it was just chance, or maybe another trap. "Do you think that was the enemy?"

Julie looked at her, surprised. "That they set it? That it wasn't a natural defense mechanism?"

"Why would the ferns need that defense? We haven't seen anything big enough to do too much damage."

"We don't know what we haven't seen," Julie said. "Remember those footprints? Look, maybe the ferns are carnivorous. Maybe there is a big herbivore that chews on the branches. I do know we need to change the simulations of planet landings when we get back."

Pen bit the inside of her lip to get her mind to focus. It didn't matter why the ferns had attacked. Jocaster needed to know that they could. "Okay, we go as fast as we can. We can't fall into a trap, but we can't stay separated from the others."

"There's one over there," Julie said, her voice steady.

Pen looked at her. How could she be so calm? Then Pen saw Julie's hand tremble as she pointed out the pile of fronds. Through the faceplate, her face was ashen.

Pen grabbed the locater and stared at the screen. "They are less than a kilometer ahead. The reading is strong."

Julie looked over her shoulder. "Maybe the ferns are dampening the signal. Now they are too busy with Ariel to do it?"

Pen took one last look around. The fern they'd just left looked like any of the others. Were they all dangerous? "I don't care. Let's go."

The light was dimming as she led Julie forward. There were no more traps, at least none they noticed.

"IT'S PEN," she repeated in her helmet comms until they made contact.

"Good to have you back." Jocaster stepped forward to greet them. "Where's Ariel?"

Pen reported as factually as she could. As she finished

the story, she remembered that Liz had been Ariel's lover. She looked over to the group of people waiting ahead. Liz must have turned her helmet mic off, but she was shaking. There was no way she hadn't heard. "I'm sorry."

She approached Liz and stepped in front of her. "Liz, I'm—"

"Don't," Liz said, stepping away and sitting on a boulder. "I just need a minute."

"How are you going to..." Pen let the rest lie because she didn't have the words. If Liz needed a minute to get herself together, she would have it.

Jocaster touched Pen's shoulder. "We'll talk later, but it wasn't your fault."

"We need to get the survivors off this world," Pen said. "It doesn't want us here."

Loke broke away from the group and walked toward them. "We need to go now. The survivors don't have helmets and suits. They've tracked through this without protection. I need to know they are safe. Pen's right. No one wants us to stay here. The enemy, the plants, the animals, they all see us as prey."

"We'll go, but I'm not losing anyone to recklessness. We've lost our best tracker and the locaters are unreliable. No stims, and we'll rest. We'll go faster between, but we want to get to the survivors in a state to rescue them, not join them in hiding."

"Good," Loke said. "I'll take the lead?"

Pen noticed he asked rather than stated. Something had changed while she was gone. "We should be in pairs," she said. "No one goes alone."

"Agreed," Jocaster said.

"Any traps in the area?" Julie asked.

"Just the pits. I think the enemy went for speed rather than originality," Loke said.

Pen wondered if it was because they were being herded toward a bigger trap but didn't mention it. They would be alert enough to avoid anything.

"My team has some skills," Loke said. "Just so you know. We might not be a handpicked team, but we're not just combat trained."

"We lost Ariel's share of the medical supplies when she was killed," Pen said. "Do you have any?"

"Some, but we're not used to using them for major injuries." Loke nodded toward Asad. "He's holding them."

Before she could suggest they share out all the supplies to avoid a big loss, her helmet filled with curses and shouts. Across the way, Raj was on his back, sliding toward what Pen knew was a pit trap from the pile of fronds, the same kind of ropes that took Ariel tugging at his legs.

Asher hacked at the ropes, the hatchet seeming to bounce off without effect. Liz shot at the tops, but nothing stopped them. Everyone who could get close was tugging at Raj's arms, trying to stop his progress toward the hole.

Pen ran, raising her weapon as she dialed it up to high. Aiming into the shadows, she shot blindly. One of the ropes let Raj free. She shot again, and the rest of the ropes withdrew.

"Are you hurt?" Pen asked as she knelt to check his legs.

"No. We can't stay here." Raj struggled to his feet. "We need to go."

"I'll partner with him," Asher said. "I can help if he needs it."

Pen finished her own check. No broken bones. "Walk in a circle," she ordered.

Raj walked without a limp, keeping himself away from the shadows. "See? I'm fine."

Pen heard strain in his voice, but just nodded to Jocaster. He paired the teams and they started forward, Raj and Asher in the middle of the pack just in case. "It's when we get out of the full sun," Pen said to Jocaster. "What's going to happen when the sun goes down?"

"We'll keep our headlamps on."

It wasn't much, but Pen took the small comfort.

As she turned to speak to Liz about Ariel, a rope flew out of the shadows and wrapped itself around Raj's neck. Pen heard his bones break as she watched Raj fly into the ferns.

Jocaster raced toward the point Raj disappeared. Pen screamed at him to stop.

Liz charged ahead of him, shooting as she ran until Asher tackled her to the ground.

"Run," Jocaster shouted.

Asher pulled Liz to her feet and they sped out of the range of the ropes. At least Pen hoped so.

"We keep moving," Jocaster said. "Double time. Keep your eye out for traps." He motioned for Pen to get closer. "Raj had most of the medical supplies," he whispered.

14

When the fern forest parted and they came to a rocky clearing, Jocaster almost collapsed with relief. They couldn't afford all the rest they needed, but at least this spot would be safe for a fifteen-minute stop. It took more time than he knew he could spare to get his heart to slow and his breath to come under control.

Two of his team gone — not to the enemy, someone they could fight, but to a plant. It wasn't just the mission weighing on him; there were too many questions racing through his mind. Was this search for a home useless? Were there planets that would support human life, or was this one, the first they'd landed on, an example of what they could expect to meet every landfall?

"We need to keep moving," Shanna said.

At least this time it wasn't Loke pushing against his authority. "Five more minutes to regroup and then we go. We'll make better time on this terrain."

They would have to be careful. A hard-packed path might not contain killer ferns, but a fall could break a leg, or a shadow could hide this planet's version of a snake. The first sun was almost below the horizon, the second rising. He wondered if the planet was ever dark. The dim light could cause as many problems as full night.

"We need to inventory supplies," he said.

It only took seconds to pile what was left in their packs. A handful of meal packs, two personal med kits, four water containers, all full, and a full bottle of stims.

"It's enough to last for a few hours. Good thing we'll be with the survivors soon," Pen said. "Let's hope they have some food and water to spare."

"How do you know they are close?" Liz asked, her voice tight with grief. Jocaster saw the lines around her mouth and eyes that held in the emotion she couldn't let show. "Maybe we should spend our energy tracking and eliminating the enemy."

"The scanners are working," Pen said. "There's a large party, it's too far to count how many, but probably the survivors, probably a few hours from here. Unless we've found some other danger from the planet."

"At least they won't have pit traps on this," Julie said, stamping her boot on the ground. "It's open enough that we should be able to see anything the enemy has put up to stop us."

Jocaster tuned out the chatter and considered the options. There were eight of them. Two teams of four, enough to watch each other's back, and still be nimble. There was water enough to get them through a few hours. So it made sense to concentrate on getting to the survivors. "Are the life signs still moving?"

Pen glanced at her scanner. "Not since we've been standing here."

"So they are probably settled in the caves." He had to

believe the survivors had enough supplies to make it back to the shuttles. But that was a decision for when his team found them. "Any sign of the enemy?"

Pen shook her head. "It would be nice, but nothing."

"They've been here," Asad said. "Fresh chips in the rocks. Maybe we can track them normally?"

"I thought you didn't have tracking skills," Liz said.

"I know the theory, never got the hang of it," Asad said. "I figured maybe you would do the tracking."

Jocaster didn't like the smile on Liz's face at the thought of hunting the enemy. He couldn't let her go while she was still raw from losing Ariel.

"Time to make a decision, Lieutenant." Loke sneered the last word. "We're ready, just tell us what to do."

And if you don't agree, you'll just do what you want.

Jocaster shook his head. "We can't run in blind."

His one mission was to get to the survivors and rescue them. The enemy was a complication but didn't change the mission. "Share out the meal packs. Make sure everyone has water. Take a half stim each and we go for the survivors."

He saw Liz glance at the tracks the enemy left. "It's all one path now," she said. "If it breaks off?"

"If the enemy isn't running for the survivors too, we'll figure something out when the tracks split." He was more worried that the enemy would get to the survivors long before his own team showed up.

THE STIM WORKED without giving Jocaster the shakes. As he trotted beside Loke, he checked the other man's reactions. Loke wasn't showing any effects either. An hour into the run and no attacks from the enemy or the planet. Jocaster knew that the planet couldn't be sentient, it was just rocks and plants and water, but it was hard to hang onto logic in the face of Raj's death.

There were no birds here, or at least none that he saw. The light was still dimming, but they could see far enough to keep going. In the distance, he could see the darker shape of a hill standing out against the sky.

"We should be there in another hour if we don't stop," Loke said. "Maybe we should talk about how to bring them back."

"We need to see what condition they're in," Jocaster said. "It's going to be hard to run them back to the shuttles. Do you remember any other paths from your survey?"

"I've been trying to pull the data on my recorder, but it isn't detailed enough. And we don't know if all the ferns are set to attack now."

"I wonder what triggered them," Jocaster said. There was no way to safely get the answer.

"I wonder how many of our people got taken on the way to the caves," Loke said.

"We'll know soon enough," Jocaster said. He glanced back to beckon Pen to his side.

"I don't like being out in the open like this," Pen said as she arrived.

"You are welcome to try running in the cover of the ferns over there," Loke said, pointing to the border of green. "But, yeah, I feel like we're being watched."

"How are the life signs?" Jocaster asked.

Pen held up the screen. Jocaster saw a blob of light that indicated the survivors. He hoped it was the survivors, but it could just as easily be a group of the enemy. He pointed to a few random blips on the screen. "What are those?"

"I'm trying to tune it in more, it's hard to do that on the move. It could be scouts making sure they're safe."

Without more information, everything they were doing was based on guesses. That was dangerous. Jocaster waved for everyone to stop and huddle.

"What?" Asad asked. "We're getting close, why are we stopping?"

"We can't just go rushing in," Jocaster said. "Just because the enemy isn't attacking doesn't mean they're gone. Pen, try to tune in the life signs more. Liz and Shanna, go to the edge of the ferns and test to see if they're going to attack in case we need to find cover."

"Two of us isn't enough," Liz said. "Asher would be helpful. I'm the smallest. They can tie a line to me and pull me out of danger if needed."

Jocaster didn't want to send anyone that close, but it was the only way. "Okay, be careful and be ready to come when we call."

"How long?" Asher asked. He dropped his pack and pulled out a length of cable.

"Five minutes."

Jocaster watched them run to the edge of the harmless-looking ferns. Turning to the group, he said, "We need a plan. I don't want us to split yet, but when we do, it should be fast, no discussion. This might be the last time we have a chance to talk it through."

"A plan other than charging in from the most obvious path?" Julie asked.

Jocaster joined the laughter. "Well, this mission is only successful if we all survive."

"Do you have a plan?" Loke asked. He tapped on his recorder. "I don't see any option for getting back to the shuttles other than the way we came. The survivors won't all make it through those attacks."

"Will they have weapons?" Jocaster asked. "Maybe on

the way back, we can be more aggressive. The enemy will be gone. We could burn our way through."

"What makes you think the enemy will be gone?" Julie asked. "We could be running for our lives on the way back. The enemy could be building more traps."

"If we don't destroy the enemy before we head back, we'll be easy targets," Pen said. "Don't forget we have to make more than one trip with the shuttles." She typed something on the tracker pad. "When we get closer, I suggest we split into two groups. One will go after the enemy and the other to the survivors."

"You are assuming the enemy will gather at the caves?" Asad asked. "What if they're split? Some at the shuttles and some ahead?"

"Then we have two fights on our hands. At least we'll get reinforcements when we have the survivors." She sighed and stopped fiddling with the tracker. "Hey, maybe the ferns got all of the enemy and there's no one in our way."

Jocaster saw Liz running toward them, Shanna and Asher trailing her.

"No attacks," Liz said. "I took a sample of the tree and nothing happened. There must be more than one kind of fern."

"Okay, we can skirt that ones we know are deadly." Jocaster didn't like the risk, but the priority was getting the survivors. "Pen's idea is good, any other suggestions?"

"My team goes for the survivors," Loke said. "They'll know us."

"Not just your team," Jocaster said. "You, Shanna, Asad, and me. Pen and Julie will go for the enemy to gather intelligence. Asher and Liz will scout traps around the caves."

"Maybe we can set a few of our own," Liz said.

"Just don't get caught," Jocaster said.

Asher bent to retrieve his pack and static blurted from the communicator. He grabbed it and tapped three keys that cleared the signal.

"All come to my location." The transmission was clear and unbroken and the same enemy voice.

"I obey." Four responses, then silence.

"Five enemy. Nice to know. And I guess that's our signal to speed up," Loke said, holding out the bottle of stims.

Jocaster nodded. "Another half. But don't get complacent. There could be more of the enemy than responded. Stay close now. We'll split up when we get near enough to see individual life signs. That way we can use the private comms to stay in touch." Jocaster looked at the locater screen. "Pen will tell us when that happens and then report for her team. I'll be the comm for my team, Liz report for you and Asher."

Pen juggled her weapon and locater unsuccessfully. "I need to be in the center of the pack so I can focus on the life signs." She slung her weapon over her shoulder.

"One question," Liz said. "The enemy was speaking standard. There's no reason for them to want us to overhear that message. It would be more effective to surprise us when we arrive."

"How can you be sure what the enemy is thinking?" Loke asked. "Maybe there are only two of them and they are making it sound like more. Maybe they forgot to turn off the translator. Maybe they don't care about what we hear."

"You seem to know more about them than we do," Liz said. "Can't you even guess? Are you trying to help us or not?"

"I want the same as you, to find my family and get the hell off this planet before we all die," Loke snapped. "We're wasting time. Even if I knew the answer, would it help?"

"We won't know until you tell us," Liz said, taking a step closer.

"Shanna? Asad? Am I hiding anything? Do you know some secret that will make this shit storm stop?"

"We don't," Asad said. "We wouldn't keep a secret like that. We told you what we know. The battle was fast, and we were trying to stay alive, not make an intelligence report."

"Enough!" Jocaster stepped between them. "Let's go."

Loke moved to run beside Pen. Jocaster placed Liz in the front.

Stims didn't just burn out bodies. They played with the control centers of the brain. Irritation would flash to rage without warning. Jocaster knew his suspicion of Loke was more likely a result of the drug, not for any real action on the man's part. Knowing didn't make the feelings go away. He would watch Loke closer until they were safe.

15

As much as she wanted to, Pen couldn't stare at the locater screen all the time. The stim was making her attention jump around and there wasn't enough interest in her surroundings to fill the gaps.

The survivors were still about an hour away by her reckoning. It would be a while before the life signs would resolve into anything clearer. She just needed to keep peeking at it for indications of the enemy.

"How will you know when to split us up?" Loke asked.

Pen shrugged. "I guess, when I see it I'll know. I want to be really close before we do it. No point in taking the risk if we're all going in the same direction."

"You okay with only Julie?"

She grinned. "Yeah, I think it's better if Jocaster is with you when you find your people. Julie and I will be fine." She glanced at the screen. The blob of light indicating the survivors was resolving into patches. "Still no sign of anyone but the survivors," she added.

"They're good at camouflage," Loke said. "We didn't know they were there until the ship attacked."

Pen shifted her weapon on her shoulder and glanced toward the ferns. They were running closer to the cover now that the plants seemed more benign. The feeling of being watched hadn't passed, but at least there was a place to run for cover if something happened.

Loke knew more about the enemy than he was saying, Pen thought. He never seemed surprised at what they heard. Never seemed to wonder about anything. Maybe some less direct questions would dig something new out. "What did you see when they attacked?"

He looked into the distance without answering. There was nothing to see but more hard packed, dry dirt and some kind of rock face. Pen waited.

"We were preparing for the rendezvous," he said. "You would have loved the party we set up. I haven't seen my people so happy in many years. We were going to link up and find a home."

There was pain and loss in his voice. Remembering how she'd felt when the news came, Pen couldn't imagine what torment Loke bore.

"The alarm went at the same time their missiles connected. A lot of shaking. Then people started screaming. Not just in the same room, but all over the ship. The comms were jammed with the sound of terror and death."

"They boarded you right away?" Pen kept her voice low, not wanting to break whatever mood made Loke so talkative. She noticed Asher and Jocaster slowing their run to close the gap.

"Their missiles did enough damage. I'm guessing we lost half the crew to hull breaches or electrical bursts." There was moisture in his eyes, but no tears fell.

"Did you see any of them? The enemy, I mean."

"Not then. Not alive. We had composites made up from

all the data we could find. Messages from other lost ships. Reports from scouts who'd had near misses."

"You had scouts outside the ship?" That never happened on *Dark Prospect*. The only time anyone went outside was when engineering needed to fix a broken sensor or something. "How did they survive the near misses?"

"Yes, we had scouts outside. Not on that day, but most days at least one scout ranged ahead," Loke said, still staring at something ahead of them. "They didn't survive longer than it took to transmit their report."

That was a piece of information the captain could use. "How…" She was going to ask how they missed the evidence that the enemy was close but realized there was no good way to word the question.

Loke glanced her way and then turned to face ahead. "How did we miss the signs? It's okay. I ask myself that every day. The scouts who got attacked were a long way out. We thought they'd covered their tracks. We were desperate for information."

"And?" Pen asked. "If I'm going to be spying on them, it would be nice to have an edge."

He turned to her again. Pen could see fury and pain in his eyes. "They're vicious. They'll kill you without a thought. They're cunning. They give no quarter. Don't let them know you're near. If they find you, shoot."

There was more, Pen could sense it. Would he keep talking? "How big are they? Do they have natural defenses? Is there a weak spot?" If she only got to ask a few more questions, then there was no reason to hold back.

"You'll know when you see one, don't worry. As far as we know, they are bipedal, much like us. No one has seen one outside the combat suit. For all we know they aren't organic life. They could be robots. They could be anything. There's a reason they want to annihilate us, but I don't know what it is."

After that outburst, Loke moved away from her. There would be no more information. She checked the locater. The patches of light were fading into individual dots. "We'll be splitting up soon," she said into her helmet comm.

The team shifted position so that each small group was together and ready to go.

"We need to see the entrance to these caves," Jocaster added. "There's a break in the ferns. We'll scout there first."

The team channel went dead. Jocaster signaled for her to go to the command channel that only he and Pen shared.

"What's the secret?" she asked.

"Why does Loke know so much about the enemy?"

Pen resisted the urge to look over at Loke. "Don't you mean, why don't we know anything about them and he knows so much?"

"Yeah, something's wrong. When we get back, we need to talk to the captain."

It wasn't the right time to argue, but Pen worried that the captain knew as much as Loke and just kept it quiet.

16

The gap in the ferns wasn't the entrance to the caves as Jocaster hoped. Pen said the survivors were close, like on the other side of a thick wall, but they couldn't blast through because they could kill anyone on the other side — and they didn't have explosives.

Jocaster crouched in the shadow of a large boulder, the rest of the team were scattered around other rocks. Not exactly hidden, but good enough. The blue stone was warm from the sunlight which was now almost gone, replaced by a dim glow from what Jocaster thought of as the night sun.

"Five life signs around the next bend," Pen said. "They flicker, but definitely close. Maybe they set guards?"

"I'll go look," Shanna said. "If it's our people, they know me."

So much for the plan. We did get a break while we talked, without anyone fighting to keep moving.

"No one goes without my order," Jocaster said. "We stick together as much as we can until we find the entrance. Loke, you go ahead and see who's waiting for us. Pen go with him. We'll stay close in case you need help."

"I won't let him get near enough for that," Pen said.

Jocaster watched them creep around the pile of rubble that obscured his view. Staying behind waiting for information was agonizing, but he was in command and that meant behind the front lines.

"It's not guards," Pen reported.

"The enemy," Loke said. "I can get at least one of them."

"No," Jocaster said. "Unless you can get all five, don't try. Are they guarding anything?" Five enemy soldiers explained the placement of the traps, a few sent in different directions could create a lot of pits with the right equipment.

"No," Pen said. "I think they might be searching for the entrance to the caves."

"What do they look like?" Asher asked, violating protocol by cutting into the communication.

"Tall," Pen responded. "Taller than you, Asher. Unless their armor disguises them somehow. They're in combat armor, well padded. They don't seem to know we're here. Maybe their locaters don't recognize us."

"Can you record them?" Asher asked.

"No," Jocaster said. "It's too dangerous." Jocaster wondered if Asher had other orders. Or maybe it was just his initial suspicions of the man amplified by stims.

"A little intelligence might help all of us in the future," Asher said.

No matter the danger? Jocaster wouldn't let Asher's agenda, imaginary or not, interfere with the mission.

"We need to survive to send any intelligence over. It's not the time," he said.

"If you've finished the debate," Loke said. "How about I reduce their number. If I take out one, the rest of you can shoot. We have greater numbers."

"How were you planning to get through the armor,

Loke?" Jocaster asked. It was more to make sure the man wasn't disobeying his order to stay put than anything else.

"There's joints," Loke said. "Hit one hard enough and it will take off an arm or a leg — or a head."

"So they're humanoid?" Jocaster felt some relief at that. He'd been worried that the enemy was some kind of giant roach or came in a shell they couldn't penetrate.

"Yeah, maybe," Pen said. "Can't count on them having the same weaknesses, but Loke's got a point. Blowing off extremities will likely kill one."

"And bring the rest to us. The odds are too close. If we had ten to each one of them, I think we'd still be at a disadvantage," Jocaster said. "The only way around this mountain is in that direction. Otherwise we're climbing in the dark to bypass that slide we saw. Head back here. We need to follow them."

"They'll get to my family first," Loke said. "Just let me get closer and I'll kill them all."

"Don't be an idiot," Shanna broke in. "You'll be dead and probably get us killed too. Your family needs you alive."

Loke came into sight, abandoning his plan without comment. Pen followed, walking backwards to protect him.

The next step seemed obvious, so Pen didn't know why Jo hesitated. "We split up like we planned," she said on the command channel. "At least me and Julie go."

"Give me a minute," Jo said. "I didn't expect to stumble on them so quickly."

"We don't want to lose them," Pen said. She could feel the urge to go back in her whole body.

"We also don't want to fight them right now." He indicated they should go back to the team channel.

Pen stepped closer to Julie, ready to head out as soon as she convinced Jo that she was right.

Julie gave a tiny nod and hefted her weapon.

"Things have changed a little," Jo said. "We can't go looking for the entrance with the enemy parked in our way. We need to draw them out."

"Julie and I can do that," Pen said. "Then we can observe them."

"No. We need you gathering intel," Asher said. "Sorry, I meant that as a suggestion. Go ahead, Jocaster. I mean, Lieutenant."

Jo closed his eyes, a sure sign he was annoyed. "Jocaster is fine, Asher. You are a civilian. Please don't issue orders again. Here's the new plan. Asher and Liz, you'll draw them away. I'm hoping all of them will go. Pen and Julie follow them, get intel, and report over the team channel. The rest of us will wait until the path is clear, or we'll deal with any of the enemy who stick around — somehow. Then we'll keep looking for the cave entrance."

He glanced around, clearly expecting someone to try to argue. Pen had nothing to offer, and felt a relief that Jo finally issued orders.

"Okay. Julie and Pen get into place. Asher and Liz, wait for them to report before acting."

Pen led Julie to the same point she'd observed with Loke. Leaning around the rock, she checked that nothing had changed. "Crap," she said. "There's only three now. I don't know where the others went."

"Give us two minutes to get in place," Asher said. "We'll make it seem like something blew up. Maybe we'll get lucky and the ferns will take the enemy down."

"Pen and Julie, hold up and let Liz and Asher get set. Observe the three in front of you. When the coast is clear, you start looking for the missing enemy," Jocaster ordered. "Keep your chatter on the private channels."

Pen checked her helmet timer. Two minutes felt like an hour, but right on the second, a blast came from the ferns at the edge of the rocky ground. Static blurted in her helmet. It looked like the three enemy soldiers were asking permission to investigate. One standing erect, the other two looking into the distance as if they could see through the ferns. And maybe they can, Pen thought.

"What if they don't go?" Julie asked. "Killing them is bound to alert the others."

"Let's see what they do," Pen said, moving her hand to hold Julie back.

Whatever they were waiting for came through. All three of the enemy soldiers raced to the source of the blast.

"I hope Asher and Liz got away," Pen said. "We need to check the campsite fast for trails."

"I'm not as good as Ariel," Julie said.

"Maybe we don't have to be," Pen said. She hoped there was a nice, clear trail that didn't lead to a trap. If the situation was reversed, she'd make sure that anyone trailing would fall prey to every pit and rock fall that she could set up.

The ferns were about a hundred meters away. As soon as the third soldier passed into the cover, Pen sent Julie to the far side of the camp. They walked the perimeter looking for signs of a trail.

"The only rock chips I see are heading around the mountain," Julie said.

"Yeah. I think they must have stopped here, but I can't tell if they came across from the ferns or around the mountain." If they crossed from the ferns, it was good. If they came this far and stopped, it meant the entrance might be a long way around. "Any sign of the survivors?"

"No. You?"

"No, and that worries me." She kept her gaze on the line of ferns in case the three soldiers returned. "Maybe we just missed a clear path from the crash site?"

"Fingers crossed," Julie muttered.

Pen switched channels and made her report. "Give us time to get ahead of you, Jo. If something goes wrong, I'll feel better if you're not in the middle of it and can come to our rescue."

"Five minutes," Jo said. "Asher and Liz have got the attention of the enemy. They're leading three away. That makes six enemy, not five, so be careful there's not more. If we can stop them responding to orders, we might have a chance."

JOCASTER LISTENED to the stream of reports from the two teams. Having them on the command channel allowed him to filter the information before passing it on. Things moved fast, and it took him time to get the rhythm of it all.

Asher and Liz were still drawing one of the enemy soldiers away. The other two were trapped for the moment, or Jocaster hoped they were since no one was watching. They may have escaped.

Pen and Julie were trailing the other two soldiers, too far to gather any real data, but Jocaster wouldn't let them risk getting closer. He didn't trust that the enemy couldn't see them.

"Last one knocked out," Liz reported. "Should we circle back to the first traps, or join you?"

"How did you manage that?"

"Even with a helmet, a well-placed rock will do some damage," Asher said. "Should we try to remove the helmet? It won't take too long."

Jocaster hated missing the opportunity, but it was too dangerous. They didn't know that the enemy was really disabled.

"Join us. We'll have noticed if they got out of the traps."

"Pen, any reaction from the two you're following?"

"No. I don't think they can communicate with each other over distance. Maybe that dampening effect wrecked their system, too."

It hadn't stopped their commander bringing them together, Jocaster thought. "Just be cautious. Their comms might start working."

"I don't think they know where the survivors are," Pen said. "I think they are in the same position as us. And that's nowhere. We haven't found any trace of a large group of people passing, and by now we should have unless they got very lost on the way."

Jocaster had been worried about the same thing. "How are they searching? Do they have scanners?"

"Not that we can see. One of them is looking at the ground, the other is looking up the face of the rock."

"What does your scanner say?"

There was a pause and then a curse. "We've passed them. How can that be? Even if they're moving deeper in for safety, we should have found the entrance by now."

"We're going to wait for Asher and Liz," Jocaster said. "Keep going and report anything you see."

"Okay. Just be careful. There are some places with no cover along the way. It looks like some kind of massive rock fall in other places. The ground is unstable because of all the shards."

"That'll slow us down," Jocaster said. "Remember that when you come back. We'll probably be farther than you expect."

Jocaster waved his team to stop. He updated them with Pen's report. "Could there be some kind of equipment that survived the crash with the survivors? Something that would help them hide the entrance, or cover their tracks?"

"Like a glider or a hover transport?" Loke asked. "Don't you think I would have mentioned it? No. The escape pods were not equipped with anything more than survival gear: meds, food, water."

"Then how did we miss the entrance? How did the enemy miss it?" Jocaster waited while Loke and his team thought it over.

"There are trackers in the group," Shanna said. "At least, I'm assuming some trackers made it."

"Good trackers know how to hide a trail as well as find one," Loke said. "Who's your best one?"

"Ariel," Jocaster said. "No one else was close. She would have thought of it sooner, but now that we have, maybe we'll be okay."

He tapped the command channel. "Liz, how long before you get to us?"

"Five, maybe ten minutes. We went in the opposite direction from you."

"If you were hiding a trail, what would it look like?"

"Shit, I should have thought of that."

"And I should have taken the locater from Pen," he said. "Forget that, what should we be looking for?"

"On the rocky ground? Look for places where it might have been swept. Brushing away the chips would stop someone following. I'll look for signs as we go, but unless we cross the trail, we won't find anything."

"I'm sending Shanna and Asad to look at where we've been," he said. "When you meet them, just keep coming."

Liz acknowledged his order and closed the channel.

"Loke, we'll keep going forward," Jocaster said.

"Ask Pen about the life signs," Loke asked as they trotted along the path. "Are they still strong?"

Jocaster tapped the command channel, but there was no response. No static, no clicks. The channel was dead.

17

"Can you get Shanna on the comm?" Jocaster asked, hoping the problem was in his equipment. Losing contact with them while they were so close to the enemy churned acid in his gut.

He saw Loke's lips move behind his faceplate, but nothing came through on the team channel. *Is he talking to Shanna? Or is he trying to get me on the comm?* His heart sped up courtesy of the stims and anxiety. If Pen was in trouble, he needed to get there fast, and every second standing here felt like an hour.

"No," Loke's voice came though his speakers on the local channel. "Looks like we're back to short range comms again."

"Or, maybe Pen and Julie have been taken," Jocaster said. "We'll leave the trail checking to the others. Let's go."

"Jocaster. We can't change the orders if we don't have comms." Loke stopped moving. "Pen and Julie knew it was dangerous. They would be on alert for traps. We haven't seen anything sophisticated from the enemy."

Jocaster stopped, not wanting to run out of the range of

the comm channel, realizing how alone that would make him feel. "Maybe that was just a setup. Maybe they didn't care if we fell into the traps. Maybe—"

"Slow down. Don't let the stims take over. The enemy fell for the tripwire Asher and Liz set up. They didn't expect us to fight back. They're not worried about us. I'm guessing they're heading for the survivors and they'll kill us later."

"The ones we trapped could have reported in. We don't know if their comms are affected by this problem," Jocaster said. "Look, we need to keep going because standing here isn't getting us closer to our people or yours."

"Fine, you go rushing in," Loke said. "I can take care of my part. I'll check for the entrance and you go find out if Pen and Liz need rescuing. If anyone else checks in, maybe you can tell them about the change to orders." He started forward, gaze moving between the boulders that lay at the bottom of the rock face and the path to the right.

Jocaster knew he couldn't break his team again and hope to keep control. He barely had control of himself. If Loke was sounding like the reasonable one, he needed to take a step back and think. He didn't have time for that; he only saw one option. "Compromise. We go a bit faster and I'll check for signs of trail clearing while you check for entrances."

"Fine," Loke said.

Jocaster thought he saw a flash of relief on Loke's face. No one wanted to be alone out here.

"They've stopped," Pen whispered. Even knowing that the comms were secure, she couldn't bring herself to speak out loud this close to the enemy.

"Can you see them?" Julie asked as she flattened herself against the rock face beside Pen.

"Yes, they're wearing helmets, but I think the faceplates are open. I can hear that they are talking, but no idea what about."

"Get back here," Julie said.

Pen realized she'd been inching forward as she tried to listen. Two more steps and she'd be visible to the enemy. She looked around for cover. The usual skirt of boulders was missing in this section of the cliff. As her gaze moved past Julie, Pen saw a fold in the stone. She would be hidden from the enemy, but still be close enough to see what they were doing. About fifty meters back, the last boulder cluster jutted into the path.

"Get behind those rocks," she said, pointing. "I'll stay here until we know what's happening."

"That's at the edge of the comm range," Julie said.

Pen gauged the distance. "There's no other cover," she said. "I need you to be safe if I'm caught."

"Safe?" Julie laughed. "There's no safe place here."

"Relatively safe then. Just go and see if the comms still work," Pen said. She gave Julie a shove and then twisted her body into the cleft. The two enemy soldiers were still talking, so she hadn't lost any advantage.

"Am I coming through?" Julie asked.

"Yeah, a bit staticky. Don't go any farther."

"Same back at you," Julie said.

In the silence that followed, Pen tried to interpret the actions she observed. One of the enemy spoke into his wrist, probably communicating with the three trapped soldiers, or whoever he'd spoken to before.

The other leaned against the rocks checking weapons. The two soldiers were identical from her perspective. Same height, same wide shoulders, same stance. Maybe it was training and the suits, but it was eerie. They may be humanoid, but no humans looked that identical. It made her more determined than ever to see their faces, or whatever they had.

"Anything?" Julie asked.

"No. Well, they are having no luck with the communications. One of them is trying a bunch of different things, but no one is responding. I take that as a positive for our side."

"Do you think they've found the entrance?"

"Hard to say. They aren't going inside anywhere, and don't seem to be guarding anything. They just keep trying to talk to someone." Pen glanced down at the locater in her hand. "The survivors are close now. The entrance should be right around here."

"Okay, what do you want to do? Attack? It's a pretty even fight."

If they didn't manage to kill these two soldiers in the attack, they were dead, and probably everyone else, Jocaster, the rest of the team, and all of the survivors. "Pretty sure it's not an even fight unless there are three of us to every one of them — and they are already halfway dead. I'm guessing they've actually killed. We've just done simulations. There's a difference."

"Are we going to sit here until they move on? What if they decide to camp for the night?"

"I'll report in. If Jocaster is close, we'll have reinforcements." Pen switched channels without waiting for Julie to respond. "Jocaster?"

Nothing.

She blinked the volume up. "Jocaster, I'm reporting in."

Nothing. And this time Pen noticed how dead the

channel sounded. It couldn't be a range issue; they were plenty close enough. "The channel is dead."

Pen wouldn't put words to the other possible reason no one was answering. They had to be alive. She couldn't do this without them.

"Get back here, Pen. We need to talk," Julie said, as if she was in command.

Pen leaned forward to see if it was safe to leave her hiding place. The two soldiers were looking up the rock face. She followed their gaze and saw a ledge about six meters above. Had they found the way in?

When the survivors arrived, there were so many of them that the search for an entrance would have been quicker and more far-reaching than anything her small team could do. If the entrance was above, then it was more important than ever to stop the enemy and search without worrying about defense.

"Pen?"

"Give me a minute."

The closest enemy soldier was pointing at the ledge. The other one nodded and walked back toward Pen.

Knowing he couldn't hear her didn't stop Pen automatically holding her breath. If he came close enough he would see her. She'd set her weapon against the wall when she squeezed in. There was no way to raise it without making noise.

Two more steps and he would see her helmet.

Moving back into the cleft would make noise and catch his attention. Staying put would leave her unable to move if he noticed her.

Her lungs were burning from holding in the air.

The enemy soldier bent to the ground one step before he would be on top of her.

Pen let out her breath slowly and took in another.

He was placing a tiny device on the ground. He stacked a few shards of debris over it, making sure there was a gap facing the path.

The stims boosted Pen's natural adrenaline. Without action to burn it off, her arms trembled. It would only be moments before her legs started. Then she'd have to move or collapse.

The soldier checked his setup, then turned to join the other.

He hadn't noticed her.

Pen blinked the stress sweat out of her eyes and forced herself to look at the two enemy soldiers.

The one who had stayed put hadn't exactly stayed in place. He stepped back onto the trail from the wall.

Pen looked up and saw a second device stuck under the ledge. This one was clear to see now that she knew to look, but Pen knew none of the others would think to look up.

"They're setting better traps," Pen said.

"We need to let the others know," Julie said. "Get back here."

"Go back to better cover," Pen replied. "I'll join you as soon as I think it's safe."

This trap wasn't just a pit with something deadly inside. Unless alien technology worked very differently, this was a small explosive charge that would start a rockslide. The thing on the ground must be a trigger.

Something had changed. This trap was designed to take out the whole rescue team, not just one or two at a time.

18

"We should go back and tell Jocaster," Julie said as soon as Pen rounded the rock pile she had sheltered behind.

"Then we lose track of these two," Pen said. "If we surprise them, maybe we can capture one."

"That's the stim talking," Julie said. "If we go forward, it's kill or die. There's no way we can take a prisoner."

"We need to try," Pen said, ignoring the stim comment. "I can't do it alone, Julie. We need to work together. We need to do this while they're separated."

"It's suicide."

"Maybe not." Pen glanced back to refresh her memory of the terrain. It was open. The cliff face went up, the ring of debris and rock chips was ample after the cleft, but not before. Then there was a wide, open space, like a field leading to the fern forest. "We'd have to move fast when we get to the cleft. No cover after that. Weapons out, shoot one, take the other."

Pen watched as Julie checked her comms. She was trying to call Jocaster with no success based on her reaction.

"We can at least make the trap useless," Pen said. "If we take out the first one, then it gives us more distance. And we'll know to look now."

"How can you be sure of that? We don't know what their technology can do. The only thing we know is that the enemy is very good at killing."

"I didn't mean get inside and turn it off. I meant just try to move it so we can pass."

"Can we do that without being seen?"

Pen shrugged. She knew they couldn't, but if Julie would agree to do that, then getting her to attack would be easier; one agreement opened the door for another.

"I need to see this," Julie said. "I'm not agreeing, and I'll go alone. You wait here."

"No. We go together," Pen said. "You need me to cover you. If they get you, I won't know until they come after me."

Julie banged her fist against the rock. A few chips flew off and she shook her hand. "Damn, that rock is hard." She motioned for Pen to step aside and took a look along the path. "Okay," she said.

Pen knew from the sigh in Julie's voice that she wasn't completely convinced. "You go first. I'll hold back. The cleft is tight, but doable. Maybe don't put your weapon in first like I did."

When they were in place, Julie started talking. "I'm looking. They're eating and waiting for something. Still can't tell what they look like. Facing away from me, but their faceplates must be open because of the eating."

"Are they talking?"

"Not right now," Julie said. "But they keep looking across at the ferns."

"Can you see anything?"

"Not from this angle."

"I'll risk a look," Pen said. Standing back wasn't easy. She eased from behind the fallen rock and scanned the open space. "Three more coming," she reported. "Stay put."

She grabbed the locater from her utility pack and looked at the screen. Life signs in the mountain, not moving. The two enemy soldiers shone bright, as did the three running toward them — the first time they'd ever registered. No sign of Jocaster or anyone else behind them. That was good. They wouldn't run into the situation, but it also meant they were too far back to help.

"What's going on?" Julie's voice quavered.

"You have to stay put until the newcomers arrive. Any movement right now will catch their attention."

"Okay. These two must have seen the new ones. They've stopped peeking and are now staring across. If they turn a little more, I should be able to see their faces."

"Is that the stim talking?"

"Probably, but you didn't control it, so why should I?" Julie said. "Maybe Jocaster was right to keep us off them for so long."

"They're here," Julie reported seconds later. "I'm heading back."

"No. We need to observe more." Pen checked the locater. Still no sign of Jocaster and the others. "Can we switch places?"

"There's too many of them to take the chance," Julie said. "If they look this way while I'm gone, you won't know if it's safe to come."

Pen hated the idea of getting any intelligence second-hand, but there was no way she could convince Julie that it was okay to move. Not when she couldn't convince herself. "Give me a running commentary. I'll keep quiet unless it's critical."

"Pen, I'm not getting trapped here," Julie said. "I'll do it, but as soon as I think I can leave without getting killed, I'm gone."

"Understood," Pen said, hoping it wasn't safe for a few minutes. Not because Julie would be in danger, but because they needed to know about the enemy.

"I can't hear anything, yet, but I think they are making moves to pack up and leave," Julie said. "Moving away from us, thank God."

The stim trembles were starting up again. Pen bit the inside of her cheek to keep her focus on the task.

"They are talking, but I can't make it out."

"Maybe your comms recorder will catch enough." Pen could listen on the way back to Jocaster.

"One of them is moving closer to me. He's looking at something on his wrist, so I can't see his face. He's making a report."

Pen closed her eyes, praying that the enemy would stop short of Julie's position.

"Don't talk," Julie said. "I'm opening my helmet. I think I'll be able to hear him. I'll leave the recorder going."

Then silence.

Pen forced her feet to stay planted in place. The flood of stim-boosted adrenaline pushed at her resolve. Her body demanded flight or fight against sense.

Without her comms, Julie was truly alone. If something happened, if she was attacked, Pen wouldn't know. Unless Julie screamed, and then it would be too late to save her.

Pen checked her helmet clock. It had been two minutes.

Three minutes.

"I'm coming back," Julie said.

Pen went cold as relief replaced terror.

"They're going forward," Julie said. "We should head back to Jocaster with our news."

"And what news is that?"

"I can talk and run."

Julie set a pace that helped burn off the excess stims, but Pen knew it would result in an energy crash, and more stims. They would need detox by the time they got back to the ship.

"They were talking standard again. It's not to scare us, Pen. They talk standard."

Was that the news? It was good, but nothing they could use against them. And nothing they could explain.

"I heard half of the report," Julie continued. "He was taking orders from someone on a ship. I don't think they get to discuss much. A lot of 'I obey' and stuff like that."

"Any idea what the orders were?" Pen asked.

"Capture some of us for torture so they can learn more. Kill most of us. You know, pretty standard enemy action."

Pen's foot slipped on a patch of broken rocks. She'd been listening and not paying attention to the path. "Slow down," she ordered.

Julie's foot went out from underneath her and she landed on her butt. "Damn. That hurt."

Pen reached for her hand to help Julie stand.

As soon as she put weight on her foot, Julie winced and pulled out of Pen's grasp. She swore as she landed on the ground. "I've done something to my foot," Julie said, voice strained against pain.

"Can you keep going?" If she had to carry Julie, she wouldn't get far. Waiting for Jocaster and the rest to find them was going to be agonizing until the stims wore off.

"I don't think anything is broken," Julie said. She put

weight on the damaged foot and sucked in a breath. "It's bruised, I think." She took a step and limped. "It all works, it's just really painful."

Pen reached into her pack. "When did you last take a stim?"

"Two, maybe three hours ago," Julie said. She looked at Pen. "I can take a pain block. Just keep an eye on me. I might decide I can fly." She laughed.

Mixing pain medication and stims could do that. Julie's body would feel nothing as they ran, and the stims would be pushing her to go harder. But they hadn't taken a high dose, and the stim would be wearing off soon. "Promise you'll listen if I tell you to stop?"

Julie saluted. "Yes, ma'am."

"Okay. Let me know when the pain stops, and we'll get back on the run."

"So, there was one thing I still have to report." Julie struggled to sit without using her injured foot. When she was down, she stretched her legs and tried to move her feet in circles. Only one obeyed.

"Your report?" Pen asked.

"Yeah, so I said I didn't think they got to discuss orders much, right?"

"Hard hierarchy," Pen said. "Not great if the one giving the orders isn't qualified."

"Well, at the end, he must have gotten an order he didn't like. I heard him say 'Should we be risking our only home, all of our people?'"

"Like they are the last of the enemy?" Pen leaned against the rock face.

"Yeah, like we take out these guys, and their ship, which is somewhere up there waiting, and we're done fighting."

"*Dark Prospect* will be arriving soon," Pen said. "We need to get back and make sure they aren't taken out by the enemy. I'm not sure we'll be able to destroy them, but something has reduced their numbers."

"Yeah, one ship couldn't have taken out so many of ours when we were so spread out."

When Pen's voice came over the team channel, Jocaster came to a stop and blew out a breath that suddenly felt too big for his lungs.

She came into sight a moment later. "Report," he ordered as soon as he knew his voice would be steady.

"Get Julie taken care of," Pen said. Then she rattled off the facts.

Liz used some of the precious medical supplies to bind Julie's foot so it wouldn't swell more. It would have to do because they didn't have anything to repair it.

"How close do you think they are to the survivors?" Loke asked.

"Can we take them? All of us attacking?" Liz asked.

"Stop." Jocaster cut through the babble. "They've told us what they know. We can't work off guesses — any more than we are now, anyway."

"So, Lieutenant, what do we do?" Asad had picked up some of Loke's sarcastic attitude.

"Keep going as we were. We can move faster now that we know the enemy isn't hunting us — yet. They're likely to get to the entrance before us, so maybe we'll need to fight. I don't want to do that unless it's necessary. We need our strength for rescue. And, let me be clear about this, I don't want anyone accidentally forcing the issue. If we do it right, we could capture one of the enemy. We need way more information than an interpretation of what Julie recorded."

"They'll torture our families," Loke said.

"So we go now," Jocaster said. "Asher, keep trying to contact *Dark Prospect*. They need to know what's waiting for them."

"They won't be in range until tomorrow," Asher said. "Tomorrow, ship time. I've kind of lost track of the days here. No night makes it hard to judge time passing."

"Just keep trying," Jocaster said.

He nodded to Loke to take the lead. He set a faster pace than Jocaster would have. Jocaster chose not to say anything. If Julie couldn't keep up, she would say so. "Pen, hold back with me. We'll pull up the rear for a while."

Pen, already settled in the middle, jogged out of the way and slowed to join him.

He couldn't let Pen keep running on her own initiative, but there was no way he'd reprimand her in public. He turned to face her. "Go to command."

"What do you need?" Pen said.

"I need you to stop running off on personal projects," he said.

"What do you mean?" Pen sounded truly confused. "I was supposed to get intelligence. I know I didn't find the survivors, but what we got was big."

"This time it worked out," he said. "But you could have gotten Julie killed."

"She might have fallen anyway," Pen said.

"You know exactly what I mean. Going back when all

the enemy was gathered. If it had gone sideways, we could have all been dead. We would have no warning; the survivors would have been on their own."

"You told me to get information. Isn't that the mission?"

"Our mission is to rescue the survivors and get them aboard *Dark Prospect*."

Pen was silent. The woman Jocaster knew would be thinking it over. This new Pen? She could be trying to find a way to make it his fault, or to make it seem less critical. Jocaster didn't like not knowing, but he waited for her to speak.

"Sorry," Pen said. "I took a risk. No. I made Julie take a risk."

So she was still the old Pen under the defiance.

"You were out of communication. What should I have done with the opportunity? Just so I don't get it wrong the next time."

Jocaster tried not to read criticism into her words. Pen had always been blunt, the stims made that more pronounced, and his dosage was making him paranoid. "Wrong depends on the outcome, I guess. Just think it through more. Remember we need to stay free to complete the mission."

"Okay."

Now that he was finished with the conversation between Lieutenant and combat troop, Jocaster could be a friend again. "Why do I feel like you are pulling against me?"

THAT QUESTION HURT. She needed some of the credit, but not at the expense of their friendship, or the mission. It all seemed petty now that they were on the planet and everything was trying to kill them.

"I guess I didn't think of that," she said. "I'm not, you know. You're the leader. I don't want to take that away."

"That's what's confusing," he said. "I know you wouldn't undermine me, but it feels like you are."

"I said I was sorry," Pen said. If she told him, would he think she was jealous? It wasn't that. He deserved everything he got, but she deserved promotion, too. She deserved recognition.

"Just tell me what's up."

"Fine. I feel like I'm seen as your shadow. I want to move up in the ranks, but I don't think the captain recognizes my skills." There, it was out. She didn't feel any relief because when she said it aloud, it sounded just as petty and jealous as she feared.

"Am I hogging the glory?" he asked.

"It's not you."

If she thought she could get away with it, Pen would turn off the comm channel. If it was possible, she'd wind back the time and start over. Her fears were not Jocaster's problem. And when Julie told her about the enemy report, it had sounded like her future: always taking orders, never giving them.

"Say something," she said. If he wasn't talking, she couldn't figure out how to fix it.

"I was just thinking. Trying to see it from your point of view. Hang on."

Jocaster switched to the team channel. "Loke, a slower pace, please. You'll burn us out."

"We can take more stims," Loke responded.

"Let's not make it so we have to eat the bottle. The enemy are still looking for the entrance. They aren't traveling fast. We can't just barrel into them because we're racing."

Pen watched Asad's back, waiting for him to slow. It took a minute, but the pace dropped from a sprint to a slightly slower sprint.

"Thank you," Jocaster said. He transferred to the command channel. "I guess I see that maybe the commanders see us as a team, not as individuals."

"Yeah. A team led by you," she said. At least he wasn't telling her she was making things up.

"If only they knew," Jocaster said. He laughed. "I think it might be more that I have seniority. I did win the game before you."

"One session before," Pen said.

"Still gives me seniority. I might get the credit for what we do right, but I also get the reprimand when it goes wrong."

"Fair enough. But I get to be invisible no matter what."

More silence.

"It might be my fault," Jocaster said.

"No."

"Let me finish. I might have been protecting you. If they knew the truth, we might be having a different conversation. I guess protecting you when your plans go off track reinforces that you are a follower."

Pen didn't know he'd been doing that. "Oh. And when a plan is successful, I try to give you credit. So, it's my fault, too."

"To be fair, Pen, my plans usually go right. Yours not so much." He laughed again.

"Oh, that's because yours are so safe, and mine are spectacular." She said it as a joke, but the truth was that her plans were riskier. "Does that mean I'm not a good leader," she asked, "because I try for the high result?"

"You deserve the chance to prove it one way or another,"

Jocaster said. "From now on we work on that. We take credit or reprimand for our own actions. No more protecting or sharing credit."

"Okay. So, I'll be better on this mission. I've been taking some risks so I can get some credit."

"Yeah. That's where you're being crazy. We'll all get credit if we're successful. If we fail, I don't think there's any reprimand for the dead."

20

J ocaster crouched beside the opening in the rock face, the only one they'd come across the whole time. It must be the right one, but there was no sign of the enemy, and no traps. The enemy was ahead of them. How had they missed it?

"What are you waiting for?" Loke asked. "We've searched for long enough. Maybe the enemy is already inside."

"One more minute," Jocaster said as he stood to rejoin his team.

This could be the last time they were together. Jocaster wanted to see the faces of the people he was taking into the mountain.

"Helmets off. We can talk." He waited until everyone finished wiping the sweat away and orienting to the dim light. The first sun still hadn't set, but the world was cooling as the light dimmed.

Seeing faces helped him know how tired, wound up, or strung out each one was. The information would be useful when it came to deciding how to pair up and deploy them.

Now that they had been one team for hours, he realized that they could have all come from the same ship. No matter whether their skin was dark like his, or almost translucent like Julie's, they were all pale from lack of real rest. Most of the faces were tired but determined. They would get through whatever was ahead. Only three caused concern; all from his team.

Asher was so calm that it gave Jocaster the creeps. But maybe that was good. He wouldn't go crazy when they got inside. Liz was grieving. He could imagine how that felt, no refuge to deal with it until the mission was over. It worried him that something burned behind the grief: rage?

And Julie. Her stare was too intense. She almost vibrated with focus. And there was no sign of pain from her injury.

"Julie, how's your foot?"

"It's good. I mean, it will need attention when we're done, but it's not slowing me down. I'm good to go, Lieutenant."

"How many stims have you popped?"

"Enough."

So many she's lost track.

"We need someone to guard our escape. Julie, that's you."

"No. I'm coming in." Julie took a half-step toward Jocaster, lifting her weapon a fraction.

"Can we afford to leave someone behind?" Asher asked. "We can't just leave Julie, she'll need a partner."

"I told you I'm coming," Julie said.

If they survived, he'd make sure that simulation training contained a lot of arguing about orders. Jocaster held up his hand. "We can't debate everything. As soon as we step through that opening, things are going to go sideways. That's the only thing I can guarantee. Let's not assume the enemy missed the opening. They're inside. There's no trap because they didn't know how close we were. We're going in together. My plan is to kill the enemy if they get in the way of taking the survivors out. If I tell you to do something, do it."

This time when he scanned the faces, Jocaster saw only determination. The weariness was gone, if only for a while.

"If we kill the enemy," Loke said, "we only have to survive the planet. I'm in."

The others nodded. Jocaster told them their positions. He would not be in the front, but he wouldn't be at the back either. Now that he knew where the enemy was, or most likely was, he couldn't lead from behind. Too many things could go wrong before he knew what orders to give.

KALIN STOOD FACING what looked like a solid wall. The target was inside this mountain but may have come in through another entrance. He couldn't access the scanners on the orbiting ship because the rock interfered. That meant they had to rely on what they could see, feel, or hear. They would be vulnerable without helmets, but that was his only choice other than blowing up the wall. Without a clear understanding of the stability of the mountain, doing that could kill everyone nearby, including him. Before he used explosives, Kalin needed to be sure there wasn't an opening.

The rock inside was confusing his sensors. The multicolored strata pixelated the image on his helmet. There was a low rushing of air that dulled his hearing in the speakers and gave no hint to source or direction. The suit's gloves weren't sensitive enough to feel the rock, so they would be stowed. Before taking the risk, he needed more information.

"Riam, helmet open, report what you see," he said.

Riam obeyed. She leaned close to the wall and reached with her hand to touch the surface. Then, replacing her helmet to activate the comms for privacy, she said, "It's not flat, but it's hard to see the surfaces."

"What did you hear?"

"Just that damn wind."

Kalin motioned for them to retract their helmets. When his was sealed into the collar of his suit, he tried to focus on hearing over the susurration. There were no other sounds, but the wind must be coming from a direction.

"Take off your gloves," he ordered Riam. "Feel the rock."

She slipped her gloves into the pocket on her right leg, then tentatively placed her hand flat against the rocks. "Warm."

She pulled her hand away and Kalin saw blood. "Was that the rock?"

"Yes. It is sharp. Only a few scratches. I will be capable."

He had no doubt that she would. Soldiers obeyed until they were dead.

A sound came over the wind. Voices, from the entrance.

"Feel the wall. There may be a hidden entrance," he ordered his team. "I will deal with the intruders." A little blood now would sharpen their senses for whatever came at them.

He crept toward the entrance. Yes, now he could hear them chattering. How they learned his language he couldn't explain, but they were still outside. There would be time to slip deeper into the mountain and set traps if his team found a way through.

Decai approached. "Kalin," he whispered. "We have found a way."

He waved his hand for silence and listened again. The

intruders were still talking. They hadn't heard Decai. Kalin slipped back to his team. "Show me."

The wall folded back two meters to the right of where they stood, the pattern of the strata causing an illusion of solidity. Kalin gestured for Riam to lead the way and the others to follow. He would be the last one through, giving him time to find a way to stop the intruders.

He couldn't destroy the entrance, as it might be the only way out, but he could make it appear that he had.

Kalin stared at the roof. Perhaps the confusion he saw in his scanner would affect the Adversary, too. There was a cluster of stalactites between him and the entrance. Kalin set his weapon to beam and shot at the grouping. They glowed but didn't fall.

He set his weapon to projectile. The intruders would hear him shoot, but the risk was small that they would rush through the opening and see him step through.

He sent a spray of slugs into the roof. This time the stalactites fell, shattering as they landed. It wasn't perfect, but it would slow the intruders, and if the shards were as sharp as the wall, they might take some damage as they struggled through it.

He turned and found the opening. His team was waiting for orders a few steps in. "Go. We don't have much time."

21

S hots from inside stopped Pen as she moved toward the entrance to the mountain.

"Hold," Jocaster said.

"Why?" Loke asked. "The enemy is right there."

"Let's not walk into their bullets." Jocaster gave Pen the signal to look.

She bent at the waist, so she wouldn't take a head shot if the firing started again. Looking into the gloom of the opening she had to squeeze her eyes shut for a moment to adjust her eyes. "Rubble, but no people."

"Then we go," Jocaster said. "Helmets sealed. Keep low."

"Walk carefully," Pen said on the team channel. "This stuff is scratching my suit. If you fall, you might not get up." She eased to the back of the space. It was a domed cave with no other exit. Well, none to be seen, but someone had been here shooting, and they weren't now.

"My suit is cut," Julie said. "Loke, will the survivors have any kind of protection?"

"No."

"We can't bring them out through this," Julie said. "We'll have to find a way to clear it."

If they didn't kill the enemy, Pen thought, they wouldn't have time to deal with it. "Should we bring the shuttles closer?"

"No time, and we'll have to leave people here, remember?" Jocaster said.

His no arguing order didn't stop discussion, but Pen wondered how much discussion he'd put up with before it became arguing. "Then our mission changes a little?"

"You mean to kill the enemy first?" Jocaster said. "If we can capture one, it would be helpful, but yes. Priority is making sure we can take the survivors home. So, the enemy needs to be neutralized."

"How do we get out of here?" Loke asked, staring at the rock face.

Asher stepped forward. "Do we have any life signs?"

Pen checked the locater. "The survivors, still nothing on the enemy. They must have a way of blocking us. I've only seen them on the scanner once."

"Can you set it to scan the rock?" Asher asked, reaching forward. He pulled back his hand. "It's almost as sharp as that rubble."

"Why?" Asad asked. "Outside, we can touch it and walk on it."

"Erosion is my guess," Shanna said. "It doesn't matter. We don't have anything to deal with cuts. If you touch the wall, you'll have to live with it."

Pen kept her eyes on the scanner as she listened. The wind dulled the sound of their words, which probably meant any sounds of the enemy approaching would be dulled, too. Her scanner was cutting in and out, but there was some kind of void to the right. Then her screen went black.

"We're on our own," she said. Pointing to the void, she added, "It's there. But I don't know if anyone is lurking."

JOCASTER HAD to remind himself to breathe with every few steps. There was no sign of the enemy as they cautiously moved along the passage, but they couldn't move without lights, and lights signaled their position to the enemy. For all he knew, the enemy could see in the dark.

The only good thing was the rock had lost its optical illusion. The walls were pale red, splotched with deep gray. Jocaster took off his glove and touched the rock with his ring finger. No cuts. They could feel their way if necessary.

"Hold up," he said. "Turn off your lights."

In the sudden dark, Jocaster closed his eyes and counted. When he hit twenty he cracked them open. There was light around the turn. "Look ahead, Loke."

He watched Loke bend to peek around the corner. Nothing shot at him.

"A big cavern," Loke reported. "I saw three exits. No enemy, no survivors. Maybe we'll find a clue when we get a closer look."

And maybe they'd walk into a trap. Jocaster moved to the head of the line; he needed to see for himself.

Loke nodded toward the other side of the opening, two meters at least away. "I can get there, if you cover me," he said. "Two angles are better."

"You cover me," Jocaster said. When Loke was in place, Jocaster rushed across. There was nothing to hide behind. He pressed into the wall and hoped that stillness would disguise him long enough to see something of value.

"Careful of your suit," Pen said.

"It's not sharp anymore." Jocaster slowly looked through the space before him. Then at the walls. He reached out to grab a strand of fabric caught on a rough patch. "What would the survivors be wearing?"

"Whatever they had on when the attack came," Loke said.

Jocaster passed him the threads.

"The enemy were in combat suits," Loke said. "This is proof the survivors came through."

Jocaster nodded. "I don't know if the enemy had time to set traps. We'll go in. Stay alert."

He held back as the others slipped past. Until he was sure there were no other openings to the tunnel, he would assume the enemy was behind and he needed to be ready for an attack.

His team spread out in the cavern, checking the walls and three exits for signs of trouble or survivors. "Pen, any indication of what direction the life signs are?"

"The locater is just a lump of plastic right now," she said.

"Any clues? Anyone?"

"All three exits show evidence that someone passed," Julie said. "The survivors must have explored the whole area before finding a place to hide."

"The enemy set one trap I can see," Asad said. "Just a small rockslide tripped by bumping one stone. Would have hurt someone, but nothing fatal. I guess they're afraid to block their exit. And it's not like they have a big head start."

"We could set our own traps," Loke said. "Something fast that won't block the passage."

Jocaster stepped into the space. It wasn't large, even though it seemed so from the tunnel. Maybe as large as the auditorium on *Dark Prospect*. It would hold a few hundred people if they squeezed. "We need a clear path," he said. "Your people need to be able to run through if we don't manage to kill the enemy."

If we're all trapped here, we're dead. And Dark Prospect *will arrive not knowing the enemy ship is orbiting until taking the first blast.*

"We can't just stand around," Julie said.

"Double check each exit," Jocaster said. "If we don't have to split up, we won't."

"Two are clear," Asher reported. "The one in the middle is booby trapped. We won't all get through, but one or two people could."

"So much for the enemy not having a lot of time to set traps," Liz said.

Jocaster heard frustration and fear in her voice, both echoed in his gut.

"It's possible this was set by our people," Shanna said. "They've been here longer, and it would make sense to build defenses. They don't know for sure we are coming."

"Good point," Jocaster said.

A friendly trap will kill just as effectively as an enemy one.

22

If it was the enemy, why only booby trap one tunnel? Jocaster could only think of two reasons. To delay them finding the survivors who were down that tunnel, or to herd them somehow into a more lethal trap.

"Check the signs again," Jocaster said. "If we can find a way to avoid going down false leads, we'll get to the survivors faster."

He motioned for Pen to join him. "Is the locater any help?"

"I would have said if anything changed," she answered. "I don't know if we can avoid going down all three exits." She shrugged. "Maybe they all lead to the same place."

"I'm thinking we might be able to disarm that trap from inside." He didn't want to separate the team again but couldn't see another way to complete the mission. "I'd prefer it if we could get through and reset the trap. Then we might be able to force the enemy into it."

"You're worried that we won't be able to communicate, right?" Pen was watching the rest of the team as they searched the tunnels for clues. "If we stay together, we're one target."

"I know, but if the communicator goes down, we can't coordinate."

"You have to trust us," Pen said. "We need a contingency plan for loss of communication, and then we need to get going."

"You think Loke is about to take his people and go?" Jocaster asked. He'd been watching Loke since they entered the mountain. He seemed to realize the value of the team, but how long would it last?

"If we split, I want Loke with me," he said. "And his team broken up, so they don't do anything crazy."

"Okay," Pen said. "What about if the comms go down?"

"Like you said, we need a contingency." He didn't think the question was if the comms would go offline, but when.

"There's nothing," Loke reported. "I don't like the idea that my people went through the separate tunnels, but it looks like that's exactly what happened."

"We might have three parties to rescue," Jocaster said.

"There is something," Asher said. "I think the trap was set from inside the tunnel. The enemy went down that one. We just don't know if they did it because they knew the survivors were there, or whether they needed to stay together and just picked at random."

"If it was a guess, and a wrong one," Loke said, "then they'll be back."

"You said maybe a couple of people can go through?" Jocaster asked as a plan started to gel in his mind.

"There's a narrow gap," Asher replied. "I'm too tall, but most of you will be able to fit."

"Okay," Jocaster said. "Three tunnels, three teams. We wait to see if the trap can be disarmed from the rear. If not, everyone keep track of where you are so we don't end up running back through it."

"What happens if we encounter resistance?" Liz asked. "Kill any way we can?"

When they got back, Jocaster was sending Liz to counseling. Meanwhile, he could use Asher's skills if it got too bad. "Kill if you need to, elude if at all possible. If you engage, you may not survive."

"If we don't engage, it will be the same end," she said.

"Pen, you, Shanna, and Julie are going through the trap. Be careful. Loke, you're with me, we'll head to the left tunnel. Liz, Asad, and Asher head down the right tunnel. We keep the team channel open. If comms fail, you stay on mission and meet back here with any information in an hour. If you have to head back to the shuttles, leave a message somewhere we'll find it."

"Just to confirm, the mission is still to find my people and get back to the shuttles?" Loke asked.

"Yes, but Pen's team will look for a way to neutralize the enemy, since it looks like they will be following." He nodded to Pen to go through the trap.

Jocaster watched as they eased through the gap in the tripwires. He motioned for Asher to come closer as they all waited for Pen to report. He opened his faceplate, Asher followed his example.

"Liz is wired for revenge," Jocaster whispered so the other's helmets wouldn't pick it up. "You need to keep her from acting on it. I can't put you in charge, you know that, right?"

"Yes, I'm a civilian. You can't put Liz in charge either. I'll have no way of tempering her reactions."

"Asad will lead. You'll need to watch him, too."

"You've made a risky mission much more interesting,"

Asher said with a smile. He closed his faceplate and stepped toward his team.

The man was definitely weird, Jocaster thought. He passed on the order to Asad and Liz.

"How long do you want us to search for a way to release the trap?" Pen asked.

"If it's not right in front of you, just go on down. Good luck, people. See you back here safe and successful."

"IT LOOKS LIKE WE WERE RIGHT," Julie said. "The enemy came this way."

Pen glanced where Julie pointed. A scuff on the bottom of the wall. It looked like it was a drag mark from a weapon.

"Be careful," Pen said.

Julie sounded calmer, but the stims would still be driving her. As long as she didn't feel pain, she'd feel invincible. That could get them all killed.

"If we take the enemy out," Julie said, "we can take our time finding the survivors."

"We find them as fast as we can," Shanna said. "We're here for them, not for the enemy. Have you forgotten the mission? Or don't we matter?"

"Stop the chatter," Pen said, afraid that Julie would share her feelings. "Keep safe and keep looking for a way to the survivors."

The tunnel led them straight forward and slightly down. It was a relief that there weren't a handful of branches to confuse the search. From the helmet channels, Pen could hear the other teams reporting the same uncomplicated path. So far, the comms were clear and stable. She wondered if Jo and Asad were getting the same bitching on their team channels.

"There's no cover if we do catch up to them," Julie said. "No point in going slow. We should speed up. Be on the offensive. Start shooting as soon as we see them."

"And if we race toward danger, we might miss a side tunnel, or shoot the wrong target," Pen said. Then, because she wanted the mission over as soon as humanly possible, she added, "We don't have to be this slow, though."

"The tunnel is steeper," Shanna said. "We're pretty far underground now."

A quaver in her voice betrayed her feelings about their position. Pen missed the feeling of space on the surface. When they'd first landed she'd hated knowing there were no walls keeping her safe, but now it felt like the mountain was just waiting to crush her. In theory, so was space outside the ship, but she was raised there. Being underground felt alien and that meant danger in Pen's mind.

23

"There's someone ahead," Loke said. "I can hear footsteps."

Jocaster signaled him to stop. "Not enough noise to be your survivors," he said. The sound was faint, but not because of distance, Jocaster thought.

"The enemy?" Loke asked. "Do we go after them?" He sounded both hopeful and impatient. Revenge for the attack and fear for his family fighting it out.

This was the first time they were close enough to the enemy for a fight to be probable, and unlike the last time, the enemy had to know they were there.

"Our only other option is to turn around, and that doesn't get us anywhere." Jocaster reported to the two team leaders. "We've found the enemy, maybe not all. Use caution. We're going silent until it's safe."

There was cover along the tunnel in the form of rubble. Jocaster guessed that some time, not so long ago, there was a collapse. Not enough to close the tunnel, but enough to leave piles of debris scattered along the walls. Cover that would help them stay hidden, but it would do the same for the enemy.

"We go forward," he said. "Turn off your comms and open the helmet. We'll hear better."

"If we catch up?" Loke asked, still on the helmet channel.

"Depends," Jocaster said. Removing the helmets meant they couldn't discuss anything in case the enemy heard, so he'd let Loke ask his questions now. "I think we have to draw their attention to us. If it's all of them, we'll have to retreat. There's no way we can kill five heavily armored enemy soldiers without knowing their weak spots for sure."

"So, if the odds are less than two to one, we attack?"

"If we can observe first, we do that." Jocaster wanted to know more about the enemy and was willing to take a few risks to do it. Any information they could take back to the ship would be valuable. "If not, we kill. If they see us, or look like they are thinking of attacking, we shoot first."

"That's the only way we have a chance." Loke flipped his helmet open and stowed it.

Jocaster nodded for him to lead, then followed silently. They ran on the balls of their feet to minimize the sound with weapons raised and ready to fire.

A few meters ahead, the tunnel veered to the right. Loke leaned against the wall and looked around before continuing.

Jocaster followed and saw light fade ahead as the tunnel turned again.

Loke sped up.

Jocaster had no way of slowing him down. They were passing places where the enemy could have left guards. Or there could be a hidden entrance to where the survivors had settled. Had Loke's priorities changed? Or was he convinced that the only way to escape was to leave the enemy dead? It made sense to Jocaster, but he regretted not being able to communicate.

At the next turn, Loke stopped to survey again. Jocaster grabbed his arm and pointed at himself and the way ahead. He needed to be in the lead.

Loke pulled his arm free and took off.

Jocaster rounded the corner as the first projectile hit the side of the tunnel. He dashed behind the closest piles of rock. Loke was just ahead of him, firing back.

Two of the enemy stood in the center of the tunnel, blocking their way. They were firing toward Loke and Jocaster but didn't seem to be aiming.

"They are just holding us here," he shouted. "Take them out."

"What do you think I'm trying to do?" Loke yelled back.

"Then do a better job," Jocaster said. He aimed for the knee of the enemy soldier on the right side, making a dead-on hit. The soldier buckled but recovered and stepped forward. "See? They can be damaged."

Loke's next shot hit the same soldier on the shoulder. "Small targets are harder."

The injured enemy slipped behind his companion who fired a few more rounds before marching toward them.

Jocaster fired, his shots going wide.

The enemy soldier stopped spraying his shots and aimed at Jocaster. Chips of rock from the walls and floor showered him. He felt each one cut his face. Too late to use his helmet for protection.

Loke shot the soldier, not even slowing him.

Jocaster stood and fired the rest of the ammo clip, but they all hit rock.

Then the soldier stopped dead. After a moment, he or

she or it turned, grabbed the injured one and dragged it around the turn in the tunnel.

"We can take them," Jocaster said.

When Loke didn't respond, Jocaster looked at his position. He was cradling his hand and swearing.

"How bad?"

"No big deal if we had medical supplies," Loke said. "Do you have something to bind this?" He held out his hand. A gouge ran through his palm.

"You got shot," Jocaster said.

"No. Rock chip. I leaned on it. Look."

Jocaster checked his pouches and found a strip of bandage before he glanced where Loke was pointing. "Yeah, so that's not great."

Where the enemy's ammo made contact, the rock was bright and striated. Like the entrance.

He wrapped Loke's hand to stop the bleeding. "Sorry it's not exactly sterile."

"I'll live. You look like shit."

The little cuts were burning, but there were no painkillers, antiseptic, or anything useful.

Jocaster engaged his helmet and reported to the team leaders. "The rock gets sharp when it's cracked. Take care. We ran into two of the enemy. If they split up, you might all be running into them. We injured one, not clear how badly."

He disengaged his helmet again. "You up for pursuing them?"

Loke was staring at the wall across from his position. Jocaster turned and saw an opening in the tunnel.

"We should go in there, at least for a peek," Loke said.

"And if there is nothing there?"

"The enemy are still ahead of us."

The survivors were the mission, and if they were

through that opening, they were behind the enemy. "I wouldn't count on the enemy running for long."

"You go ahead," Loke said, struggling to his feet. "They missed this opening, I'm not going past it."

"And what if the other three enemy soldiers are inside?"

"They wouldn't be waiting for us. They'd just come out shooting."

Jocaster scratched the wall so they could find their way back. "Okay, we go in."

Loke led the way through the crack in the rock. Jocaster listened for any sign that the enemy was returning, or that there was a large group of people inside. Only silence.

He slipped inside to find a short tunnel with two exits. Loke was gone.

Jocaster took two steps inside the first exit. No sign of Loke. The other didn't offer any assistance either. He regretted his decision to remove helmets. There was no way to contact Loke without yelling, and that could bring enemy fire down on him.

He snapped his helmet into place. "Asad, Pen, bring your teams back to the cavern."

24

J ocaster reported Loke's actions when the teams gathered. "We can go after him and commit to that entrance, or we can keep looking."

"We go after him," Shanna said. "Asad, you agree, right?"

"So, our mission becomes rescuing Loke?" Asad shook his head. "No. If that's not the way in, he'll come back and find us. I think it's dangerous to leave the enemy running free. And none of it helps find our people."

"We found a way in," Pen said. "It might join up with Loke's if we go down."

"Why didn't you report?" Jocaster wondered if he'd have acted differently with that news.

"You called us back. Should I have paused to speak? We only saw it then, just as you gave us the order. The mountain seems to be made of folds and tunnels that mostly face in the opposite direction you want them to. What we found could just as easily be a way out of here."

"Not like a ship," Julie said. "Not designed for our use or comfort. Not designed at all."

"So?" Jocaster asked. "We go in the tunnel Pen's team found?"

"We didn't see anything in ours before you called us back," Asher said. "It would make sense for us to find two exits. If both tunnels lead to the same place, and we go down Pen's path, that trap is going to be a nasty problem if we're on the run when we come out."

The trap could be disarmed if they had time. But Jocaster had no idea how long they had to get to the survivors. Would the enemy have risked bringing the mountain down on themselves if it went off? Were they just outside the cavern, waiting to attack?

"Check it again," he said to Asad. "Can you guess how much damage it will do if we just trip it?"

"Maybe," Asad said. "I could use some help."

"That's me," Liz said. "I aced explosives. Of course, just small controlled charges, not enemy explosives on a planet that might be alive."

Jocaster couldn't quash the idea of a living planet. They didn't know if that was possible, but it felt like they were under attack all the time.

He watched them peer at the tripwires and connections. "The other option is to split again. One team goes after Loke, the other follows the new path," he said half to himself.

"And the enemy?" Pen asked.

"We know two of them are in Loke's tunnel. That leaves three unaccounted for. Maybe they're in your tunnel, maybe not. We'll have to deal with it when it comes up. If you have to shoot, aim for the joints."

. . .

Pen hoped no one would jump on the idea of splitting up. They needed everyone together, so someone could always be on the alert. And if the side tunnel opened into another cavern with more than one exit, a big team could be split up. If it was only two, they'd have to take a bigger risk and maybe lose their only chance of succeeding.

"There's no explosives," Liz said over the comm. "The tripwires will bring down a shower of rocks, not great, and not enough to block the entrance."

"When the rocks break, they'll be sharp again," Jocaster said. "Almost as bad as explosives, and there'll be dust. We haven't encountered that and don't know what it will do to our lungs. If we're caught in the mess, suits won't protect us. When the survivors are leaving, they won't even have suits."

Pen saw Jocaster rub his forehead. Exhaustion was getting in the way of thinking. Not just Jocaster, she noticed. "I say we trip it now. The enemy will have to worry about getting slashed as much as us. We have time to figure a way through when we have the survivors, and any dust will have had a chance to settle."

"We'll have to pass through whatever falls twice, once in and once out," Julie said. "Double the risk of a cut."

"One of us only," Pen said. "You all get through and move a ways down so you're safe. Don't worry, it's not as tight as we thought. I'll stay and trigger the fall. Then I'll join you."

"Why don't we trigger it from inside?" Jocaster asked.

Relieved he wasn't objecting, just clarifying, Pen said, "We might not be able to. And if something goes wrong, we have no one on the outside to go for help."

"Like there's any help around," Liz said.

Jocaster ordered everyone to the tunnel and then told her to be careful before he followed.

Pen held her breath each time one of the team members took the first step through the trap. Julie went in first to help guide people; Liz stood at Pen's side, giving instructions. This was the third time she'd repeated them. Then she said 'good luck' and ran for the opening.

Jocaster was the last to enter. He made the same moves as the people before him. She was sure something would go wrong right now. If their luck was consistent, this was the worst time. Losing Jocaster might mean the end of their mission. The others might argue with everything he said, but they followed him. She wasn't sure anyone else would be able to carry that off.

She blew out a lungful of air as his left foot disappeared into the darkness. The trap was still in place. No enemy had burst into the cavern with weapons blazing. Now it was up to her.

Her heart thudded with each step toward the misshapen arch that opened into the mountain. It was lack of oxygen because she was holding her breath, at least that's what she wanted to believe.

"I think that wire will trip everything," Asad said, pointing to a filament high on the left side of the opening.

"Suddenly everyone's an expert. Are you planning to hang out right there?" Pen asked, making a shooing gesture. "Julie, take them to where the tunnel dips."

"Call us back if you need us," Jocaster said. "Don't be a hero. We need everyone."

She waved him away then looked closely at the trap.

The trigger wire was too high for her to reach comfortably without climbing. The trick was going to be tripping the wire and getting back out of the way before the fall started. She didn't have good enough aim to throw a stone and hit the wire. And she wasn't going to waste ammunition on it. Her solution wasn't much better though.

There were sufficient holds in the rock face to climb. The fall might hurt when she jumped back, but she knew how to roll and tuck.

Pen realized she was stalling. Placing her weapon and pack on the ground out of the way of any damage, she gave her arms and shoulders a shake to loosen them up.

Pen reached over her head for the lowest hold and launched her body upward.

Two holds got her close. One more and she'd be there. She jammed her fingers on the tiny ledge of the next hold, looking at her target. Heaved with her right hand, reached with her left. The wire twanged as she hit. She lost her grip and fell backward, and the sound of shifting rocks accompanied her to the ground.

Then it went dark.

WHEN SHE WOKE UP, Pen remembered hitting the ground and the air rushing from her lungs. Dust still floated in the air, so it hadn't been too long. She took a breath and tasted the dust but no blood. Pen sat up and rolled over to pick up her pack and weapon; the grip was slick with blood. She looked at her hand; her fingers were sliced from the wire. At the sight of the injury all the pain roared into her hand.

She forced her gloves on to cover the wound; no one needed to know she was hurt. The medics on the ship would deal with getting the glove off.

Standing, Pen stared at the entrance to the tunnel. She smiled. The enemy were very good at traps now. The hole was smaller, and the rubble covered in dust. If you didn't know better, you'd just barrel through. Then your feet would be in tatters, and you'd be easy to kill.

Knowing what was in store gave them a chance.

The dust wasn't sharp. Pen scooped as much as she could onto the debris. Enough of a blanket of dust and the jagged edges wouldn't poke through so fast.

When she was done, Pen stepped lightly through the opening. Inside she inspected her feet. No cuts.

25

Jocaster struggled to focus on the path through everything rolling around in his head. Loke might be dead, the survivors might be captive, Pen could have been killed. None of it mattered right now. Finding evidence of the survivors, if not the survivors themselves, did.

"It's getting warm," Shanna said.

"Yeah, it will probably get warmer as we go deeper," Asad said. "Better than freezing to death."

"Not if it's suffocating us," Shanna said.

Were they purposely trying to cause panic?

"Keep it down. I don't want to miss sign of your people because you have to chatter." Jocaster reached for his helmet clasps. "In fact, helmets off. We don't know if we can trust the mics to pick up any sounds."

"It feels better," Pen said, shaking her hair out. "Cooler."

Jocaster added worry about suit malfunctions to his list. "Let's keep going. This tunnel can't go on forever." They'd been moving slowly downward for the last half hour. The survivors had more than a half day head start and didn't have to worry about the enemy while they went. How far down could they be?

"Did you hear that?" Julie asked. "Voices."

Julie was in the middle of the pack. If there were voices, someone else should have heard it. No one agreed.

"It's gone now," she said, taking a step forward.

Asher placed his hand on her arm. "Just a second." He pressed his ear against the rock wall. "There's something nearby."

"Can you be more specific?" Jocaster asked.

Asher shook his head.

Before Jocaster could speak, loud pops sounded to their right. And then a rumble of rock falling.

"Keep moving forward," he ordered. "Weapons ready."

"It came from the right," Pen said. "It has to be the enemy, right?"

"Fighting Loke," Shanna said. "Please let it be that, not the first shots into a crowd of people."

"We would have heard screams," Liz said. "Hold up." She veered to the opposite side of the tunnel.

Jocaster thought Liz was preparing to defend them, when she rolled around a corner into a side opening.

He directed the others to follow. It was in the direction of the shots, and maybe the survivors. Jocaster felt some of the tension drop from his shoulders. Once they found the survivors, it was only a matter of escaping. And with more than this handful of people to lead, he could make the trip back safer and faster.

THE NEW PASSAGE WAS SHORT. Jocaster, at the end of the line, took two steps in and came to a stop. They were in another cavern. Not filled with people needing rescue, not filled with enemy soldiers ready for the slaughter. Safe for the moment.

Light filtered in from the top of the dome, meaning they weren't as far underground as feared but it was brighter than he expected. Had they been underground long enough for the first sun to rise again?

The rock here was green, all shades of green. Not in a shattered illusion, but in bands and pools of lighter color against the darker shades at the entrance. Water trickled somewhere, but the sound bounced so much that Jocaster couldn't locate it.

"Three exits, again," Pen said. "We'll need to split up."

Jocaster stared across at the far wall, where three new tunnels opened. From this distance, it didn't look like there were traps. If they kept splitting up to follow the paths, they'd run out of people soon. "I don't know that the survivors would risk breaking into smaller groups," he said. "There must be some kind of sign. Liz, you and Asad can check for evidence they passed through and report in."

He turned to survey the condition of the rest of the team. Tired, but no more than he was feeling. The exception was Julie. Her weapon wavered in her hands. Her face was white with a tinge of green — maybe caused by the light in the cavern. He sent the others to join the search for something, anything, that would narrow their choice of passages.

He knelt beside Julie, speaking quietly. "How many pain killers have you taken?"

Julie looked away, frowning. The weapon stilled for a moment as she concentrated. "I can handle the pain."

"How many stims?"

"Not enough," she replied. "Yeah, I'm living on them right now. If I don't, I'll collapse. I'll deal with it when we get back to the ship. You need me, Lieutenant."

"I need Junior Lieutenant Julie Ackerman, not a stim junkie." He held out his hand for the pills. "You know it's dangerous to administer them yourself."

Julie's hand slipped into her med pouch, but she didn't remove anything. "I can't risk being alone when I need one."

"You can't trust your judgment," Jocaster said, making it an order.

She pulled out a bottle of stims and shook it. "Only a few left anyway."

Jocaster took the bottle. He could feel some of the others watching him, too far away to hear the conversation, but his actions were clear.

He could hear Liz and Asad returning. It was decision time.

There was no right answer. If he let her keep the bottle, Julie might collapse anyway from an overdose. Water and food would mitigate the side effects, but they were in short supply.

He counted the pills inside. Five pills, enough to kill her if she didn't pace them right. Even if she did, that many would leave her with some serious damage to her nervous system. He took one pill and handed it back to her. "You make this last until we get to the survivors. When you need another, let me know. Don't be surprised if I say no."

Julie took the pill and slid it into her pouch. "I'm good for a bit. I'll break it in half. I don't want to die from it, Lieutenant. I just want to complete the mission."

"You are going to guard our exit," Jocaster said. "When we know which passage, you'll stay in here. And secure our escape."

"I need to be there when you find the survivors," Julie said. The trembles started up again. "Leaving me behind is not a good decision."

"Thanks for your opinion, Junior Lieutenant. You'll stand guard, or you'll go back to the shuttles alone. You choose."

"Yes, sir. I'll be here when you get back." She slumped against the wall and lay her weapon across her knees.

KALIN STOOD in the shadows of the passage. The maze of tunnels had slowed them. The would-be rescuers were ahead of him, closer to the people who'd fled the wreckage of the ship. His team was now reduced by two, thanks to these adversaries. Casualties were unexpected and Kalin felt emotions he couldn't name. He ignored them and concentrated on the current problem. If he did the right thing here, they had a chance to complete their orders in one swoop.

The way out would be faster now that they had passed through the maze. There would be no need to go through the twists and turns of so many tunnels. They would exit through this cavern, along the passage across from him and through the next. He would be on his way back to the ship in less time than it had taken to find the entrance.

Sola would have no reason to deny him the victory.

"Be alert," Kalin said to his two remaining team members. Killing Lachi and Imah had been unavoidable. The wounded were no use in battle.

"One remains," Riam said. "Kill her before she can give warning?"

Kalin watched the woman across from them. Had she noticed that she wasn't alone? If so, she was incompetent. No effort to hide her presence, but perhaps that was arrogance instead of stupidity. "It needs to be silent," Kalin answered. "We cannot kill her from here; the noise would give just as much warning."

"There are three of us. Even if the entire party returned, they would be at a disadvantage," Orah said.

Kalin signaled for silence. She was wrong. Lachi and Imah were dead because of the action of only two of their adversaries. Not the time to remind Orah of that. She would need confidence in the coming fight. "We watch for ten more minutes. When I am satisfied that it is not a trap, then we rush this woman, kill her and hunt the remaining Adversary soldiers to their death."

Or perhaps keep this woman captive? His orders were clear, but in battle things were not easily controlled. He would deal with that when the last of the soldiers begged for their life. "Then we will deal with the escapees."

He watched the woman across the cavern. He knew it was female by the shape of the combat suit, but it was too far for other details to be clear. These people, the great Adversary, were like softer versions of his own people.

26

Pen hugged the side of the tunnel as she approached the opening where Julie stood guard. There was no sign of her, and that had to mean trouble. She'd heard nothing that would indicate a battle, so maybe it wasn't too late.

She sidled closer and noticed Julie pacing to the side of the opening, suit sealed.

She should be hidden and resting.

Pen slapped on her helmet. "Julie, what are you doing?"

"Enemy soldiers at the entrance. I'm trying to draw them out so I can finish them." Julie walked past the opening and stood next to Pen's position. "I can't leave them lurking and I can't deal with them in the shadows."

"How many?" Pen resisted the urge to pull Julie to the safety of the tunnel; that would just confirm where her team had gone.

"I think three. Maybe the two Loke shot are dead, or maybe they're circling around."

"They haven't reacted?" Pen tried to remember if any of the other tunnels emptied behind the enemy but trying to make a map just muddled her more. It would be easier to kill them if they didn't see it coming.

"No and I don't know what to do now. Maybe lure them into a different passage?" She started pacing again. "Maybe we should just run for a separate exit. Leave the survivors to protect themselves until we can regroup?"

"Not a chance," Pen said. "We have to deal with this and then catch up. The people hiding in here are our mission. We don't go back without them, or without proof they're all gone."

"Check with Jocaster. Maybe leave Shanna and Asad to protect their people," Julie said, voice tight. "Loke went off on his own. Why should we risk everything if he's not willing to stick with us?"

"Julie, we won't leave these people to the enemy." Pen stared across the cavern. She needed to see evidence of the enemy before acting. If Julie was ready to abandon the mission, maybe she was imagining the threat.

As she watched, one of the shadows across the cavern moved. Only a little, but there was nothing moving inside to cause that change.

"The odds are too much against us," Pen said. "Slip in here and we'll rejoin the others. Then we'll have more firepower."

Julie didn't answer.

Pen turned her attention from the enemy position to check on Julie, who raised her weapon and fired into the shadows.

"Idiot," Pen said. Then she stepped into the cavern and fired as three shadows resolved into charging enemy soldiers.

No one fired back, they just kept running forward. Pen knew they were dead if she didn't do something.

Too late to drag Julie backward, too hard to aim at fast moving targets. She looked around the cavern and then shot at some stalactites hanging a few meters in front of the tunnel, hoping they would fall on the enemy and, at least, pin them down, if not kill.

The spikes hit the ground like thunder, the entire cavern vibrated with the impact.

Pen reached to pull Julie away from the cavern. Part of the floor caved in, leaving a pit separating the enemy from them.

"Come on before they start shooting," Pen ordered, hoping Julie could hear over the crashing of still-falling stone headed for the floor of the pit a long way down.

"So much for the easy way out," Julie said, limping along beside Pen. "We'll never get hundreds of people across that."

It was just one more thing they would have to deal with when they found the survivors — the ever-growing list.

JOCASTER STOOD WAITING at a bend in the tunnel, his team behind him. The shooting had stopped. Asher was on his way to find out what happened. Now that the battle was silent, he could hear the survivors again. They were close, but Jocaster had no guarantee they were going in the right direction. When he got back to the ship, he was never leaving the security of well-lit and well-mapped corridors again.

A flicker of movement far down the tunnel made him raise his weapon. Then it resolved into three people — not the enemy. Asher, towering above the other two, hurried ahead. Julie was limping again. Would he have to relax and let her have another stim?

"The enemy is trapped, but not for long," Asher

reported. "I don't know if they were hurt. Pen and Julie are fine."

Jocaster nodded, keeping his attention on Julie and Pen until they were in range of the helmet channel. "Report."

"Three enemy entered the cavern. We shot down part of the ceiling and there's a chasm between us and the exit if we go that way. The enemy will be finding a way across. They know we came down here. At least, I'm pretty sure they do."

Jocaster motioned for the team to continue forward, holding Pen and Julie back. "Anything else? Any intelligence on the enemy?"

"Nothing we don't already know," Pen said. "But Julie needs to tell you something."

"I have nothing to add," Julie said, glaring at Pen.

"Pen, just tell me. We don't have time for games."

"When I arrived, Junior Lieutenant Ackerman was luring the enemy into the cavern. Not successfully, but with intent." Pen nudged Julie as if to get her to speak.

"Ackerman, what was your plan?" Jocaster tapped Pen on the shoulder and sent her after the team. He would get the story straight from Julie. Or, he'd get it from Pen later.

Julie watched as Pen disappeared into the gloom. The farther they got from the cavern, the less light seeped into the passage. Jocaster feared they were descending too far below the surface while running parallel to their target.

"I told Pen that we should kill the enemy and leave the survivors until we have more shuttles. Or, at least, bring the shuttles here."

Jocaster knew she was whitewashing the incident. Pen wouldn't have bothered reporting a disagreement. "That might mean they die," Jocaster said. "Even without the enemy attacking, this planet is hostile."

"Well, that would mean *Dark Prospect*'s resources aren't

strained by a new hundred or so inhabitants. It would mean our own people could have children, because you know births will have to be restricted to make up for it."

"The consequences of bringing the survivors aboard is not our concern. Our mission is to rescue them."

The stims are messing with her judgment. The discussion would have to wait.

"Can you move fast on that leg?" he asked.

"I can do what's needed."

Jocaster hoped she wasn't purposely avoiding a clear answer. "No more stims. I'm sorry, but we have no more pain blockers. I need you moving with the team. We can't slow down and let the enemy catch up."

"Yes, sir." Julie moved past him and started jogging to catch up.

Jocaster peered back down the passage. There was no movement. The enemy were still held back. He wondered how other people handled someone like Julie. Did the captain sometimes want to punch a wall so he wouldn't punch a subordinate?

27

"They're coming," Asher said over the comms. "I can see movement behind us. Three bodies."

Jocaster glanced over his shoulder, trying to calm his thoughts. Anger was going to get someone killed.

He didn't trust anyone else to watch Julie, so he took on that task. He'd set Asher to watch their back. The civilian was surprisingly capable even though he had no experience. It gave Jocaster pause; what didn't he know about the man? There was one more reason Asher was the right choice, as much as Jocaster hated thinking it: he was more dispensable than any other team member.

Jocaster glanced back but didn't see anything back down the tunnel. "How far?" he asked.

"They could probably fire and hit someone from where I saw them, but I don't think they want to chance another cave-in. Maybe five minutes before they catch up if you keep moving. Can we go faster?"

Not with Julie's injury.

Jocaster wouldn't leave her behind and couldn't push her any harder. It didn't matter that she'd disobeyed and put herself in this position, he was responsible for her. "Get back here. We'll look for a place to take a stand."

"They'll see me," Asher said.

"They'll see you either way. I'd rather you were with us than stranded."

"Not complaining, just reporting," Asher said.

This tunnel was different from the earlier ones. The rock was rougher, but not sharp. Boulders scattered along the walls at intervals, as though someone had dug out parts of the mountain. His team had explored a few small caves as they passed. All were shallow and had no other exit. They were stuck with their choice now until they dealt with the enemy, or until the enemy dealt with them.

Jocaster's thoughts scrambled to pull together a scenario where the team would survive. The side caves would make a good ambush site if they could disguise their actions, so the enemy was surprised. Jocaster knew that was unlikely; if Asher could see the enemy, then the enemy could see them.

It wasn't where he'd have chosen to meet the enemy, but it was all they had.

"Look for a defensible position," Jocaster said on the team channel. "We hold the enemy here."

"Tunnel's turning," Pen said.

"Everyone, follow the turn. Hold off just out of sight."

That gives us a chance, Jocaster thought, but only if we stay close to the turn. We need to attack fast. Trying to lure the enemy into an empty passage would delay action and wipe out the tiny advantage.

PEN CROUCHED behind the largest pile of rubble. It was not enough to cover her, but it was the best she could see. She knew darkness and surprise were her best cover. It wasn't as close to the tunnel turn as she wanted, but the random piles of rock had dwindled in this passage just as they turned.

The battle simulations on ship had actually prepared them for this kind of fight: exhausted, stim boosted reactions, lack of food and water, and a mission still a long way from complete. What she wasn't prepared for were the emotions. There was confidence. Her companions had all completed the training successfully or they wouldn't be on the mission. Loke swore his team was trained. And then there was the terror. No matter how confident she felt, or how much she told herself that confidence was an asset, there was a sure knowledge that this battle would result in death, not just being kicked out of a simulation.

Death meant the survivors were lost, that her ship would be attacked without warning, and she would never know if the enemy could be destroyed. And that was the third emotion, disappointment.

"Hold," Jocaster said.

Pen glanced across at Liz, who shared the point position with her. There was no responding glance because Liz stared at the opening as if it were the only thing in the universe, her weapon braced and finger on the activator.

"I can hear them," Pen said.

"You need to see them before you shoot," Jocaster answered. "If you can, hold until more than one comes into view. That way we can take as many as possible."

Movement in the corner of her eye drew Pen's attention back to Liz. She was shifting her position, creeping from around the rocks into the center of the tunnel. Through her faceplate, Pen could see Liz's lips moving. She keyed the sensitivity higher on her helmet.

"For Ariel. You'll die for her."

The words barely came through, but they repeated. It was a mantra.

Pen swore and opened the private channel. "Liz, don't be reckless."

Nothing changed. Liz, now standing in the center of the tunnel, planted her feet and touched the setting that put her weapon in rapid fire mode.

Before Pen could react, or report, a shadow entered the tunnel.

Liz flicked the activator and a stream of projectiles crossed the body. It crumpled and lay still.

If it's just a matter of ammo, Pen thought, we might have a chance.

"Jocaster," she said. "One down."

"I can see that," he said, not sounding happy. "That leaves two unaccounted for. Maybe three. Someone needs to check the body; Loke is still out there."

"Liz is charging forward. I'll follow and report. Then you head toward the survivors, and I'll get Liz back from wherever she's gone in her head and join you." Confidence again, but only in her voice. How was she going to overcome whatever madness grief had pushed Liz into?

When she was sure the downed enemy wasn't firing back, and there was no sign of the other enemy soldiers, Pen ran to catch Liz, praying that she hadn't shot Loke.

Liz was using the laser setting on her weapon to burn the body. What was left identified it as one of the enemy, so Loke was still out there.

"Stop." Pen reached to touch Liz on the shoulder. "We could find out something from the body."

"They killed Ariel. That's all I need to know."

The body smoldered, and Pen's helmet had trouble filtering the stench of burned metal, plastic, and flesh.

"It's done." She touched Liz's shoulder again, hoping the contact would break her focus on eradicating the body. "We need to get back to the others."

Liz took a step forward. "You go ahead and join them. I'll take care of the body."

Pen couldn't leave Liz. They needed to know where everyone was so shooting first wouldn't end up killing their own. Jocaster was right, having Loke wandering about was a complication.

"I said we are both going." Pen used her command voice. "That's an order."

"You aren't the mission leader."

"No, but I'm a lieutenant, Ensign." Pen watched as Liz fought with the emotions tearing through her reason. "And Jocaster has every right to bust you down to Petty Officer for that behavior."

"If that's what he thinks I deserve, fine." Liz kicked the body, turned and started marching back toward the team.

Does she think she deserves a medal?

———

28

Jocaster waited, splitting his attention between the main body of his team and Pen, who was jogging behind Liz. The battle was over for now, but that didn't mean he could relax.

"Did she kill one?" he asked.

"There was definitely somebody in the suit," Pen said. She hauled Liz past Jocaster's position just as Liz was going to speak. "There's no one following us."

That was one good thing in this whole mess. Now they knew that the enemy could die, could make mistakes. Jocaster ordered them forward, covering their retreat. He would wait to find out what Liz was going to say. Maybe it would give him a way to stop her doing any more damage. If she was still bent on revenge, he would have to find a way to restrain her. The problem was he had nothing to sedate her with, and he couldn't spare anyone to guard her. Between Liz and Julie, his effectiveness was draining away by the second.

The team was closer than he expected. He asked for a

report, holding onto the protocols of leadership in the hope it would keep everyone following him.

"More fighting ahead," Asad said. "We must have under-estimated the number of enemy soldiers we were facing."

Jocaster could hear the volley of pops from somewhere farther down the passage. Then it ended. "At least we can tell where it is. If I'm not mistaken, that's where the noise from the survivors came from."

"We need to go now," Shanna said, taking two steps back from the huddle. "They don't have the skills to win a battle. They only have emergency armament. It will be a slaughter."

Jocaster reached to grab her hand and stop her progress. "It's over right now. Can't you tell? No more shots. We can't just stumble into the dark. If anyone survived, we need to do the same to save them. And if they're shooting at anything that moves, we need to find a way in alive."

"What about her," Asad asked, nodding at Liz. "Is she going to do that again? She'll get us killed."

Everyone looked at Liz as she removed her helmet. Tears were rolling down her cheeks and pooling in the suit's throat seal. She sighed deeply. "I want to kill them all, but one evened the debt. One of ours, one of theirs."

Jocaster didn't believe she'd suddenly finished grieving, or that she would have more control next time, but he felt safe leaving her without a close guard. He had his hands full with Julie, who might sabotage them. If Liz went off the rails, at least she'd take out the enemy and not their team.

"I'd like to interrogate one of them, if possible," he said. "Or learn something from a body."

Liz wiped her face with her arm. "I'm not putting anyone at risk just to satisfy your curiosity."

That was insubordination. Jocaster couldn't punish her

now; that would happen when they were back aboard *Dark Prospect*, but he couldn't just let it go.

"You will follow orders, Ensign Pernaz. Gathering intelligence is not idle curiosity."

She glared at him long enough that he worried he'd have to punish her right now.

"Yes, sir." She replaced her helmet on and turned away.

"Head toward the fighting," he said. "I'll keep an eye on our backs. Don't stumble into a trap."

"WE NEED to make it hard for them to get to us," Pen said. Just running was going to cause problems, if not before they found the survivors, then definitely on the way back. And that itch was back between her shoulder blades, this time it wasn't her imagination. "Jo, let me and Asher do something here to slow them down. We'll catch up."

Jocaster glanced behind them again before answering. Pen started marshaling her arguments.

"We don't know they are back there still," he said, but more to himself than to her. "That one could have been alone."

He was back to over-thinking. Pen controlled her urge to snap at him to hurry up. "It will only take a minute. It'll buy us time regardless if they are there or elsewhere," she insisted. "If we know they aren't coming at us from behind, we can move faster."

"What about getting out?" Jocaster was still staring down the tunnel.

"We can't come back this way in any case, remember the chasm? One of the other tunnels will have to take us out of here."

Asher stepped closer. "We can do a lot in a minute, Jocaster."

Pen gave silent thanks that Asher agreed with her. Taking him to block the tunnel would leave Jo with the best fighters, even Julie and Liz would be more valuable than Asher in the next firefight. He held his own but lacked instinct. She hoped Jo didn't make that leap. He'd never let her go if he thought she was in danger — well, more danger.

"You have three minutes," Jo said. "If this tunnel branches, we'll mark the way we go. Don't get lost."

Pen nodded at him and beckoned Asher forward toward the bend in the tunnel. "I don't think we can chance blowing the walls," she said. "I thought we'd just push some of the rockfall together. It doesn't have to be much, just look like a barrier and resist any quick attempt to break it."

"We can't do that in three minutes," Asher said.

It didn't sound to Pen like an argument. "He's not going to come back for us. It would jeopardize the mission. Don't worry, I'll take the flak when we catch up."

"That's not what I meant." Asher came to a stop between two piles of rubble. "We can chance a few shots. If we drop some rubble directly between these, we'll be done."

Pen looked at the ceiling. It looked solid, and there were no stalactites. "I'm not crazy about dropping another ceiling. The mountain will eventually land on us."

"It's fast, anyway," Asher said.

Pen didn't know if he meant setting the barrier or the death that might result. She realized she didn't care. "Let's push these closer first." She slipped off her glove and felt the texture of the rock, wincing as the cut from the trap split again. "Maybe they'll fuse."

Asher moved some of the larger boulders to the center

of the passage while she experimented. "Not completely successful," she said, turning her weapon off. "It melts a bit, maybe that's enough. If we had more time…"

"The enemy could be just out of sight," Asher said. "Normally I would hate the idea of makeshift work, but we have no time, Pen."

She glanced into the dark again, moved to peek around the corner, then flicked on her headlamp. The passage was clear for a long way. She could just make out the pile of burned out armor that once was an enemy soldier. "Okay, just a few more rocks."

She filled the gaps while Asher moved the last two boulders. "Okay, let me warm the rocks before you hit the ceiling."

A ten second blast created a shine of melted rock. Asher pointed his weapon and shot three single bullets right above. Dust drifted down with three big chunks of the roof. There were a few gaps in the barrier, but small enough to keep someone out.

"Let's go," Pen said.

PEN JOINED them later than Jocaster ordered, but before he started to get anxious.

He called a halt to let her report. He agreed with their idea of blocking the tunnel. It was sound strategy. He felt the weight of that worry lift. It didn't make much change to his overall stress, but it was one thing less.

"The noise ahead has stopped. All of it, including the voices," Jocaster said. "We're still headed in the right direction, at least we're headed in the same direction. If they moved…"

"Don't look for problems," Pen said. "At least the shooting stopped. And with no one coming from behind, we can be more aggressive. We don't need to know what's ahead until we get there, right?"

"Another cavern," Shanna reported.

"Assemble inside after you check it's safe," Jocaster said. He turned to Pen. "Knowing just before we get there would be better than stumbling into a mess. But I get your drift. I need to stop worrying about everything and just deal with what's in front of me."

She grinned at him and led him closer to the cavern.

"Why do I feel like this is just a series of caverns that go nowhere, and that our families are not even in this place?" Asad asked. "How long can we keep going before we won't be able to get out?"

Jocaster had no answer. Would he abandon the mission when it was clear they were at the point of no return? He let the question lie in his mind. No point in worrying about something that far off.

The cavern was smaller than the previous ones. He started to feel the pinch of claustrophobia. He looked up, but this cavern didn't have the light that the other had. It wasn't dark, exactly, but without their headlamps they wouldn't be able to keep searching.

He sent the team searching for signs of the survivors and bent to scratch a star in the tunnel entrance. If they passed it again, they would know if they were going in circles. His sense of direction said they were not, but under all the rock, he wasn't confident in his belief.

"There are only two exits," Julie reported. "I saw some evidence that people came this way. I just…"

"What?" Jocaster asked.

"We're deep in now," she said. "If the survivors were searching for shelter in here, I get that they would have split up to search better. What I don't understand is why they would still be split up this far in."

29

K nowing what Julie wanted to do to the survivors made it hard for Pen to think beyond her disgust at the idea of abandoning people here. But Julie had a point. Why were they still following more than one trail... when they could find one at all? The survivors couldn't still be looking for shelter.

"We don't know," Jocaster said. "Maybe they were running from something and now they are trying to get together. Maybe these tracks are set to confuse the enemy. If Ariel was still here, she could probably read more into it than we can."

"I'm not leaving until all the enemy are dead." Liz stepped away from Julie and checked her weapon. The words were casual, but she meant them.

Pen held her breath. No one would let her stay behind, but if they lost Liz now, it could mean disaster; The team was small as it was, and losing one person could make the difference between success and slaughter. Jo triggered this. He wasn't usually that insensitive. Pen wondered what was behind bringing up Ariel's death. Maybe to distract from Julie?

"That might mean we'll all die," Julie said. "Look, we have information for the captain. It's not going to do us any good rescuing these people and coming to the surface to see *Dark Prospect* destroyed by the enemy ship."

"They aren't coming in blind," Pen said. "They're going to expect trouble."

"We haven't been here long enough to make contact with the ship," Jocaster said. "They'll be in range soon unless we've lost track of time. For now, we keep going. We don't stop the mission for personal vendettas."

"I don't care what you people want," Shanna said. "I'm not leaving my friends on this planet unless I see their bodies. I'm not leaving Loke, either."

Another threat to split off. Why wasn't Jo ordering his team to stay focused?

"We're tired and the stims are taking a toll," Jo said. "Don't let that cause problems. We aren't leaving until we know the mission is complete. As Shanna said, not until we have the survivors, or we see their bodies."

"And the enemy?" Liz asked, still looking at her weapon.

"We need a rest," Pen said before a full-blown mutiny could erupt. "I know we can't stop long, but even ten minutes will help."

"In ten minutes, we can survey this whole cavern," Asher said. "Not a rest, I know, but it's not running from danger either. It's much better than standing around counting the seconds until we can go."

Pen wondered what Asher thought they would find by looking closer, but it was time Jocaster took control again, so she didn't respond.

"Split up," Jocaster said. "Half of us go clockwise the

other half counterclockwise. Given the way this mountain hides things, it's a good idea to look close."

"Maybe Julie should rest her foot," Pen said as she started walking clockwise.

"I'm fine," Julie said.

"You will rest." Jocaster pointed to a low boulder.

Pen smiled at his tone. Taking command back was not that easy, but at least he was trying. "Don't forget to look up as well as along the walls," she called over her shoulder as she moved along the cavern wall.

"OVER HERE," Pen called. "Another passage. Someone was here."

When he reached Pen's position, it wasn't what Jocaster expected. Not enough footprints for it to be the survivors. Maybe four or five different people. "The enemy?"

Pen shrugged. "It kind of looks like our prints. But I don't know what kind of track the enemy leaves. Didn't get a chance to look at the soles of the boots." He could see she was resisting an urge to glare at Liz.

"Let it go," he said. "She'll follow orders."

"If not?" Pen asked as she looked around to make sure they were alone.

"I'll deal with it." It sounded hollow to him, but maybe Pen would buy it. If people kept threatening to leave, he might not be able to stop them.

"I'm not sure they came into the tunnel," Pen said, breaking into his thoughts. "Whoever left these prints, they might have just looked in."

Jocaster bent to get a better look at the marks. Pen was right, it looked like whoever came to that point stopped and then went back the way they came.

"I found where the survivors probably left," Asad said. "What's inside this passage?"

"We don't know," Jocaster said. "I don't want anyone running off without cover."

"I didn't tell anyone," Asad said. "I figured you'd want to take control."

"Thank you. We need to know what's down here first. I don't want to leave our backs vulnerable."

"I'll go in," Asad said. "Just tether me. I don't want to fall into a trap."

Jocaster called the others over and ordered Pen and Shanna to link weapon straps and attach them to Asad's utility belt. "Just go as far as the tether lets you," he said.

Asad slipped through the gap.

The whole team watched the temporary leash grow taut. Then it relaxed.

"Shit!" Asad stepped back into the cavern. "It's us. We came to this cavern and then turned back before entering. Probably when you called us back. Two minutes later and we might have found the survivors two hours ago."

"We have been going in circles," Jocaster said. "It seems we can't trust our instincts. We need to know more about this maze. Mark the entrance to the tunnel. Asad, take Asher and see if it leads outside. We've pretty much closed the door on going back the way we came anyway."

He signaled the remaining four members of his team to continue searching for tunnels. They were not leaving this cavern without knowing how to get out.

JOCASTER STARED at the floor of the tunnel Asad had found. It was only two meters from the one they'd entered. It was hidden from a casual scan by a fold in the rock wall. He'd only noticed it when his hand felt the gap. On the floor there was clear indication that multiple people had passed, enough to be the survivors. The floor was too hard to show which direction they'd come from. Even with all the questions, the footprints were enough to restore his faith in the mission. Now all he had to do was bring his team together again.

If Asad and Asher found an exit, all Jocaster needed was for this tunnel to lead to the survivors, not a trap. He gathered a handful of flat stones and built a marker. The uncertainty was doing more than tearing his team apart, it was stealing his confidence in his abilities. Building the tiny waymarker made him feel like he was accomplishing something.

"Here!" Liz called. "A lot of people came in through this tunnel."

"More over here," Shanna called.

Jocaster headed to Liz first. Fewer people had come the way she'd found, but too many to be the enemy or his own team. The same at Shanna's tunnel. "Mark them both," Jocaster said.

He turned at the sound of approaching feet. Asad and Asher stepped through into the cavern from what was now an invisible entrance. Jocaster yearned for metal plated walls and straight lines.

"Yes, it's a way out. Through the first cavern. If we can bypass the damage at the entrance, we can get everyone from here to the outside fast," Asad said. "The enemy would have to be right on our tails to catch us before we could hide."

Where exactly would we hide?

"We are not going to get lost again," Jocaster said. "We mark every tunnel we enter and every turn we make. We also check every bend for hidden passages, so we don't go wrong on the way back."

"Won't the survivors know how to get out?" Julie asked.

"We can't rely on that," Asher said. "It might have been luck that they found this cavern so fast. They were fleeing a threat, so it's likely their memory of the trip will be muddled."

"We'll deal with that when we find them," Jocaster said. "We mark our trail. If the enemy finds it, so be it. We know we can deal with them now."

"What about Loke?" Shanna asked. "The mission is to save the survivors, does that mean we leave without him if he doesn't show up?"

"Just focus on your friends and family members," Jocaster said.

"That includes Loke," Asad said.

"We'll figure it out when we get to the main body of the survivors." Jocaster pointed at the tunnel he'd marked. "That's where they left the cavern. Head out."

Jocaster kept glancing behind as they moved through the mountain. He wasn't sure what he was looking for, but he couldn't stop.

The enemy had gone silent, maybe still trapped in the maze of tunnels and caverns. The people ahead of him were doing a good job of marking the few entrances to side passages — most of which were hidden from anyone traveling in this direction. He felt good about realizing that. Maybe his tracking skills were getting better.

The only real threat he could see was the lack of cover. If the enemy did come this way, there was little to use for defensible positions. The battle would happen in the same place as the survivors gathered in waiting. If this wasn't the way to the survivors, and the tunnel didn't change, they would walk into their deaths, not just theirs, but the survivors, the people on *Dark Prospect*, maybe the rest of the ships, too.

Just ahead of him, Julie slowed. Jocaster moved past her to see what had caused the change. Then he heard it. Noise made by a large number of people, murmuring and shifting sounds. The tunnel bent as it came closer to the sound. More encouraging, a gentle glow emanated from beyond.

"It's them," Asad said over the team channel.

"They don't know it's us," Jocaster warned. "We can't just barge in, they might start shooting."

"I'll go," Asad said. "Helmet off, hands raised, unarmed. They won't hurt me."

Jocaster nodded and took Asad's weapon. "Be ready to duck."

Asad laughed, and stepped toward the bend in the tunnel.

"We could set a trap here," Pen said, surveying the walls and ceiling.

"And block our access?" Jocaster asked. "You just like blowing things up."

"I mean when we've talked to the survivors, if they know another way out," she said. "And who doesn't like blowing things up?"

Jocaster was grateful that Pen still had a sense of humor.

Asad stepped into view. "It's safe."

Jocaster entered the cavern and had to put his hand on the wall to brace himself. It was ventilated and lit from a hole in the roof far overhead. The two hundred or so people they expected was an underestimate. There were at least three hundred here. The adults pressed their children behind them, prepared to take whatever was coming. A few people lay on the ground toward the back, injured, not dead.

Several weapons were pointed their way. No one seemed afraid, just determined to fight to the end.

He knew this was a good outcome for Asad and Shanna, as more of their friends and family had survived. It was bad for the mission. The risk doubled in his head that something would go wrong on the shuttle trips back to *Dark Prospect*. The more round trips, the higher the risk of an accident, or an attack.

He shook his head to clear his thoughts. It didn't matter how many people were here. The mission was almost complete. They'd been searching for what felt like days for these people and now he just had to get them out and off the planet.

"Good to see you again, Jocaster," Loke said as he walked away from a cluster of people, waving at the survivors to lower their weapons.

Asad and Shanna were running toward people who held out their arms.

"How long have you been with them?" Jocaster asked.

"It took me about half an hour to track them. I understand that was luck on my part. They searched for hours and only found this a little while before I joined them. Your team is still together, I see. I'm glad I waited for you."

"We took some hits," Jocaster said. "If you have any meds for Julie, she's running on stims and I'm not sure they'll have much effect."

"We can help with that. And we have food, water, ammunition." He waved over an older woman. "This is my mother. She's a doctor." He sent her to check Julie's injuries.

"How many?" Pen asked, stepping to join them.

"There were three hundred to start. They lost people

getting here but not many. It's going to take a while to get to the ship."

"The enemy will find us soon," Pen said. "Is everyone ready to move?"

"Pen's right, we need to go. You can grieve later," Jocaster said.

"We lost more than a few people. We lost everything," Loke said. "It won't hold us back, I promise. Get something to eat and drink. When Julie is fixed, we'll go."

"Good, the sooner I get off this planet the happier I'll be."

30

"The enemy is still on the hunt," Pen said.

Did Loke think they could outrun the threat? Not with these civilians.

She scanned the crowd again, assessing ability. Most of them were past the point where running was an option.

"We have people keeping lookout," Loke said. "It's not safe to stay here long."

"Fine." Pen wasn't sure that it would help. "Maybe we should organize groups? Not just run out in a mob."

"You mean sort people into most likely to survive?" Asad asked. "We aren't leaving the wounded to fend for themselves."

Pen sighed. Somehow in her heart, she'd expected the mistrust to fade when they found the survivors. Maybe it would happen when they were aboard *Dark Prospect* and someone else's problem.

"No," she said. "I meant to make sure the people who need help have it. Don't you have evacuation drills? If we all just go, the people who are hurt or slow will get left behind.

If there's a threat, everyone might panic. We break people into groups and assign buddies for the weaker ones."

Asad blushed. "Sorry. Can I blame it on stim withdrawal?"

"Sure," Pen laughed. She was willing to take the apology no matter what form. "It would help if we had food and water to soften the stims. When we get back to the shuttles, there'll be plenty for us. Until we get to the ship, anyway."

Loke's mother approached them with a jug. "Julie's foot will be okay. I've wrapped it, but she shouldn't stress it. She needs rest and time for her body to flush the stimulants." She passed the jug to Jocaster. "There's food and water. You all look like you need it."

Pen's thirst woke from its coma and she almost grabbed the jug as Jocaster took a deep drink. He held it out and she took it.

"We'll pack what we can carry. That's most of what's here," Loke said, joining them. "Whatever we can't needs to be consumed or left."

Pen passed the water jug to Asad. "I'll get us organized."

"No need," Loke said. "It's already happening. We know where the shuttles are. So we break into eight groups, one of us leading. We meet back at the shuttles. No one takes off until the whole group is assembled."

Who put him in charge, Pen wondered. "Six groups," she said. "Liz is in shock and grieving. We can't let her lead."

"And Julie might lead her group off a cliff?" Loke asked.

"I don't think she'd go that far, but let's be safe," Jocaster said. "Is there anyone with combat experience? We might be able to make smaller groups if we can explain the path."

"Not the fastest way, and no, none of the survivors are in good enough shape for leading," Loke said. "Okay, let's do four groups. That puts two of us in each. You take Julie, Pen takes Liz."

"This is still my mission, Loke."

Pen noticed that Jo didn't add any command to the words, just a gentle reminder.

"And I've been here for a while preparing for you to take us out." Loke straightened and took a half step toward Jo.

Pen saw Jo tense. Unless he had a better plan, he was going to blow it right when they were about to finish the mission. She searched for anything to say to break the tension.

But Jocaster didn't react to Loke's posturing. "Your plan is solid," he said. "Five groups will work better. You, Asher, Shanna, and Asad take one each. Pen and I will take Julie and Liz."

"Fine with me," Loke said.

"Loke, keep in mind that until you're given rank, you have to follow someone's lead. On *Dark Prospect*, your attitude will get you tossed in the brig, or demoted to maintenance."

"And with you?" Loke asked.

"We've been through enough crap; I'll give you a little leeway until we're off-planet."

Pen's shoulders relaxed as the two men shook hands. Maybe Loke would take the advice, and maybe he'd have to learn the hard way. At least for now, they'd stop butting heads — maybe.

She walked toward where the rest of the rescue team stood eating emergency rations like they were at a banquet. Now that they weren't on alert, her hand started throbbing. Maybe she should let Loke's mother check it out.

A flash of movement from a tunnel to her right made

her reach for her weapon. Before she could take aim, she saw it was a child running at full speed toward Loke.

"They're coming," the child said, breathing hard. "Cautious. Maybe ten minutes away."

JOCASTER TURNED TO GIVE ORDERS. Did they have time to create a trap to slow the enemy enough to be able to catch one of the soldiers? Was it worth the risk for some potential intelligence?

His thoughts stopped swirling in his mind at the sight of a flurry of activity close to the tunnel the enemy was approaching from — no idea how soon they would appear.

"We have traps set," Loke's mother said. "Good thing you're here, we didn't have any way of killing them. We just used some small charges we scavenged from some of the equipment to trap them."

He watched as one of the survivors pulled a cover away revealing a deep trench. Then they tossed a tarp and some small pebbles in place. The enemy would think the ground was solid. And it explained the shots they'd heard earlier.

"Good thinking," Jocaster said before hurrying to take position beside Pen.

"I wish we knew how many," she said.

"No kidding. They've had plenty of time to bring in reinforcements." He leaned in close. "It's more important than ever to capture one and get some answers."

Pen looked like she was about to argue. Jocaster shook his head, he'd argued it with himself enough. He had his decision and there was no time to debate.

A quiet scratch of boots on the ground brought his attention back to the tunnel. It turned to the right a few meters in. The enemy wouldn't see them until they came around the corner. Then they would be exposed and vulnerable. He wasn't going to waste energy wondering if they'd heard the conversations. He pointed to his ears and then activated his helmet.

The weapons around him were all pointed at the center of the tunnel. "Spread your aim," he said. "Loke, Julie, Asad, cover the lower half of the opening, we'll cover the rest."

He could trust everyone there to hit what they shot at. Asher was with the survivors back in the cavern along with Liz.

Pen and Shanna stood at his side. The enemy wouldn't make it to the trap if he didn't speak now.

"Try to let them come forward," he said. "Kill if you have to, but if we kill the first, then whoever is behind will still be a threat. We need information. If it's safe enough, let the enemy fall into the trap."

"What do you think you're going to get out of them?" Loke asked.

"How many are here? Are there reinforcements?" Jocaster couldn't believe Loke hadn't thought of it. "No point in escaping the tunnels into a legion of enemy soldiers. And even if we get off the planet, the enemy is still a threat to the remaining ships. We need an edge."

"We can debate it later," Pen said. "Pull back a bit, or you'll stop them coming for the trap."

Jocaster took two steps away from his position and watched Loke do the same. By the quiet sounds coming from the tunnel, there could only be a few of the enemy approaching. They were being cautious, that probably meant they didn't have backup.

Jocaster glanced around. A crowd of people cowering in the back of the cavern, or that's what the attackers would see as they reached the tunnel entrance. The attack force would be hidden for enough time. The sight of their victims should draw the enemy forward to take the final step onto the pit.

He bent his knees, ready to run toward the trap. He had to be the first to look in. He didn't trust anyone else with that, or to be more precise, he didn't trust anyone not to shoot first and cost them the opportunity.

The first soldier slid around the corner, hugging the wall for cover. It would protect him from direct fire but would restrict his sight; an advantage for Jocaster's fighters.

Jocaster held his breath. Two more steps and the enemy would see the survivors. One more step.

As soon as the soldier took that last step, he raised his weapon.

The enemy planted his feet, ready to fire.

STANDING in the tunnel made his skin crawl. He felt exposed. The Adversary were huddled in the back of the cavern, easy to destroy. He could take his time to find the last of the rescuers. Soon he could return to the safety of the ship and the comforting rule of the Holy Ones.

"Sola," Kalin said into the mic. "I have the survivors."

There was no response. Kalin hadn't expected any, but he knew better than to blindly follow the last set of orders without checking, or trying to check, first. His team and equipment would prove his attempt. "Decai, Orah, report."

"Tunnel clear behind," Decai said, his voice clear over the short-range transmitter.

"Two more tunnels to block," Orah said. Her task was to limit the escape paths.

"Attempt to contact the ship," Kalin said. "Report with my code. Targets located. Confirm orders."

"No communications open," Orah reported back.

Her response came too fast for Orah to have attempted contact. Kalin wasn't surprised that there was a spy for the Holy Ones on his detail, just a little taken aback that it was Orah. Now that he knew, he would make it work in his favor this time.

"Confirmed," Decai said. "Your orders?"

"Orah, how much time to close only one of the tunnels?"

"Finishing now," she reported.

"Stand ready to attack at the final one. My last order from Sola was to take some prisoners for interrogation." He prepared to step into the center of the entrance.

"Decai, I'm going in. The cavern is too large for me to cover alone. You be prepared to repel anyone who gets past me."

Both replied with "I obey."

Kalin realized that he couldn't see all the targets. Stepping into the cavern would leave room for some to escape if they were near the entrance. Both strategies had risk, but he counted on Decai to do his job.

Kalin took one more step and felt the ground give way.

JOCASTER ORDERED the others to keep aiming down the tunnel as he ran to see what they'd captured. He leaned over the pit and saw the enemy soldier pulling himself across the bottom toward his weapon.

He fired a warning shot toward the weapon. The soldier drew away and crawled toward the far wall. His leg was twisted in a bad direction. It might be hard to injure them through the armor, but Jocaster had no idea how fragile they were when injured. He needed to make sure the captive wouldn't die, or at least would live long enough to give him some answers.

"Pen?" Jocaster called. "Get a medical kit."

"You aren't going down there," she said, handing him the supplies. "He might be faking."

"We can't leave him there. I have to take the weapon, at least."

"If you're going to talk all day, let me," Liz said.

She dropped her weapon. Pen tried to grab her, but something had weakened her grip. Liz shook her off and jumped into the pit.

Jocaster watched her grab the enemy weapon and toss up it to Loke, who was standing across the trap. The survivors were crowding in, some calling for the soldier's death.

"Wait," Jocaster said. "We need to know how many there are."

"That won't take long," Liz said as she reached for the enemy's helmet.

Jocaster, afraid that she'd use the opportunity to kill him in revenge, jumped in to join her.

He pulled her back and ducked when she swung her fist at his head. "Stop."

His order found a way through her emotions and Liz went limp.

"He might be booby-trapped," she muttered.

"Probably not," Jocaster said. He kept his eyes focused on the soldier. "They don't think they'll get captured or killed. Why take the risk?"

"I don't know how they think," Liz said.

"We'll find out soon." He glanced up at the crowd. "Can I trust you to stay?"

"Yes, but I don't agree with your plan." Liz leaned against

the rough wall of the trap. "I doubt it will talk. We already know they can be killed. That's news."

"We'll never win if we can only kill them one at a time."

"Are we going to talk all day?" Liz asked.

"Just don't get in the way."

Jocaster stepped toward the enemy. The soldier batted away Jocaster's hands as he tried to twist the helmet to remove it.

The enemy touched two buttons on the front of the helmet. Gas hissed as it accordioned open.

Brown eyes stared back at Jocaster. Skin as dark as his own, the face framed with black hair in tiny braids.

This was a human.

31

Jocaster tossed his weapon to Pen and nudged Liz, who was staring at the man. He looked for guilt or remorse in Liz's expression, but there was nothing. He wondered if he would have felt different in Liz's place.

"We need to get him out of here," he said. "Help me lift him."

"No," Liz said, scrambling away. "Human or not, he's responsible for Ariel's death. I won't kill him, but I'm not helping."

Jocaster looked to see who was closest. "Asher, pull Liz out, then join me." He leaned toward the soldier. "What's your name?"

"Kalin. I will not betray my commander."

Eventually someone would get him to talk. Jocaster needed to keep him alive until he got him back. It made no sense that being human made a difference, Liz was right; it didn't change what he had done or that someone had ordered it. But now Jocaster couldn't bring himself to do what it would take to extract information.

"Were you captured and forced to fight?" Jocaster found himself asking as he realized one human didn't prove that all of the enemy were the same.

Kalin groaned as he tried to move. "No. I am a loyal soldier. You will see when my allies come for you."

"They all look like you?" Asher asked.

He reached to touch Kalin's leg, but he pulled away with another groan.

"You mean are we all human?" Kalin asked through clenched teeth. "Are you?"

This was going nowhere, Jocaster thought. No matter that the idea of humans trying to eradicate other humans was alien to him, he needed to get these people off-planet.

"Fine, we need to get you out and have a medic look at that leg." Jocaster pointed at the twisted limb.

Kalin tried to struggle to his feet, but the leg wouldn't support him. He collapsed back to the floor, no sound of pain. He kept his eyes on Jocaster the entire time.

Asher landed beside Jocaster. "If we splint the leg, it will be easier to lift him."

Loke's mother tossed down an inflatable splint and an aerosol pain reliever. "You know how to do this?"

"Yes," Jocaster said. "It won't be gentle, but we'll get it done."

Asher stepped forward and knelt beside Kalin. The pit was tight but there was just enough room to maneuver if they were careful.

"It's going to hurt," Asher told Kalin. He held out the canister. "This will kill the pain for a little while."

Kalin shook his head. "I don't trust you."

Ropes dropped into the pit beside Jocaster. "Make a sling," Loke said, tossing a tarp in. "We can lift him."

Jocaster leaned over Asher. "If you want the agony, you

can have it. We're going to splint the leg and then pull you out."

"Go ahead. I am not weak," Kalin said.

The idea of the pain he was going to cause turned Jocaster's stomach. He didn't think forcing the meds on Kalin would help when it came to extracting information. "Asher, have you ever done this kind of thing?"

"In theory," Asher said. "The leg needs to be put back into alignment. We lift, pull, and then turn until it's straight. I can do that, and you put the splint under so when I put it down, we can just close and inflate it."

"He's going to fight it," Jocaster said. "He won't be able to stop."

"It would help if he took the pain meds," Asher said. "But we can't squeeze anyone in here to hold him down."

No point in dragging it out, Jocaster thought. He held the splint ready, then nodded to Asher.

Without warning Kalin, Asher lifted the leg, holding it above and below the break. Pulling it slightly toward him, he twisted until the knee and ankle lined up.

Jocaster watched Kalin as he slipped the splint in place. His dark skin went ashy, a trickle of blood slipped through his lips as he clenched his teeth against the pain. No sound came out. He was tough.

"Close the splint," Asher said.

The splint sealed with a compound that hardened on contact with air. Jocaster sprayed a line of foam rapidly down the seam and touched the button to activate the inflation process. In seconds, Kalin's leg was encased in a rigid cast that would hold for a day or more. It would take that much time to get him to the ship and medical equipment. If he wouldn't take the pain killers, maybe he'd pass out and let them move him without resistance.

They rolled him to the side, created the sling and rolled him back. "Okay, lift him." Jocaster stood back pushing into the sides of the pit as Kalin was pulled to the surface and out of his line of sight.

Two ropes dropped in. Jocaster and Asher used them to climb out of the pit.

"He's out," Loke said. "Now what? We need to get to the shuttles."

"There's at least one more of them," Jocaster said. "He looked back in the tunnel before that final step. So, where are they?"

"You want to question him while reinforcements come?" Loke asked.

Jocaster felt Pen move to his side.

"If we just wanted him out of our way, we should have left him in the pit," he said.

"We need to take him with us," Pen said. "If we try to find out who's waiting for us to leave, it will help. Any more information will wait until we're safer."

"What information?" Loke asked. "I don't care that he turned out to be human. Him and his kind slaughtered so many of us that he doesn't get a pass."

"This is our chance to get information that might help us win the next battle," Jocaster said. *Am I only one who sees that?*

"That would be better done on *Dark Prospect*," Asher said. "He will speak there. It's only a matter of time."

His words were delivered with a conviction that gave Jocaster shivers. Was interrogation one of Asher's specialties? It wasn't in his record, but some things never made it into the official files.

"Can you get him to tell us how many of the enemy are waiting?" Jocaster asked. "Without too much delay?"

"Maybe," Asher said. "If we had some drugs... No, let's try a tactic or two. I need space."

Jocaster sent everyone away except Pen. He wasn't leaving Asher completely on his own. He trusted Pen to stop things if Asher went too far — and that's exactly what Jocaster thought would happen.

He pulled her aside. "What's wrong with your hand?"

Pen glanced at the glove. "I got a cut. It's not a problem."

"Get it looked at now," Jocaster said, reaching to remove the glove.

Pen jerked back. "On the ship. If I take it off, I won't be able to get it back on. And that means I can't help you. I'll be just another burden."

Can I order her to get help? No, she'd never forgive him.

"If it's too injured, you might not be eligible for promotion." He didn't say the worst: she might be demoted out of the ranks.

"I'll take the chance. You need me right now." She left to join Asher.

PEN STOOD ASIDE and watched as Asher began. She knew why Jocaster wanted her here and would do as he asked. But this was an opportunity for her. She'd never considered a career in shadow work, but she'd never seen it in action. Maybe it would help her to stand out, taking on these skills. She wouldn't be seen as Jocaster's sidekick any more.

It started simply enough.

"My name is Asher Jones. Our ship is *Dark Prospect*. Our main mission is to find a new home for humanity."

"You haven't been acting like that," Kalin said. "You've been... No."

"It's okay," Asher said. "I'm sure there are misunderstandings between us."

Kalin turned his head to look at the wall.

Pen didn't think trying to become friends would work with Kalin. Everything she'd seen and heard on this mission led to the conclusion that these enemy soldiers were hard and well trained.

She still thought of them as the enemy. Maybe they were human, but that didn't change what they'd done. They'd attacked and killed all but five or six hundred thousand people. History hadn't been her favorite subject, but Pen remembered that two billion people left Earth in ships like *Dark Prospect*. She knew it wasn't all down to Kalin's people, but every time they destroyed a ship, it reduced the chances of finding a home and making a future.

"You are coming with us either way," Asher said. He reached and turned Kalin's face, so they were looking eye to eye. "If we get attacked, you'll be the first to die."

"Good. Decai and Orah know I don't matter in the true battle."

Asher nodded. "What is the true battle?"

"You will know when it comes," Kalin said.

Asher turned to her, letting Kalin's head go. "Two soldiers remain. We can get to the rest of it on the ship. There are chemicals that even he won't be able to resist."

Pen swallowed the bile that rose with the light that shone in Asher's eyes at the prospect of Kalin's torture. Maybe this wasn't a skill set she needed to cultivate.

JOCASTER TURNED AWAY from the organization of the survivors. They were ready to go, but he had one more question for Kalin. Part of him said to wait and let more experienced people ask, but he knew it was a long road back and it was possible that Kalin wouldn't survive the trip.

"Is he set to go?" he asked as Asher and Pen joined him.

"It would be better if we had room on the stretchers for him, but I think he can walk on the leg with the splint." Asher looked at Kalin. "Can you?"

"I will not aid you," Kalin said as he struggled to his feet. "But I will not allow you to leave me here to die."

"We're all prepared," Jocaster said. "I just need one more answer, if you would help, Asher."

He saw Pen flinch at the question. She thought he meant for Asher to apply pressure. No, he wanted expertise, not torture.

"I will not talk," Kalin said.

Jocaster heard the pain in his voice. How could Kalin be sure he would withstand questioning?

He didn't want to argue the merit of questioning, or the process. He turned to Kalin and asked, "Are all of you human? Or are you working with aliens?"

Kalin spat and took a step, limping but mobile. "There are no aliens, fool."

"Why would you attack us? You must have known we were human," Jocaster asked.

"You said one question," Kalin said. "Do we not need to leave this mountain?"

"Jo," Pen said. "We do need to leave. This is just wasting time. They'll get all he knows on the ship."

Jocaster nodded. "He's in our group. We leave and meet at the entrance if it's safe. I want to try reaching the ship before we run."

He gave Loke the signal to start the evacuation. He and Pen were taking the final group.

32

The trip back to the entrance was fast. Jocaster regretted not exploring one more tunnel when he looked for Loke. If he had, they'd be halfway back to the shuttles by now. Another lesson? How could he possibly know when to trust someone's instincts when he questioned his own? It was in the past, and anyway, there was enough to do before they were safe on *Dark Prospect* without dwelling on mistakes.

"Where are your people?" Jocaster asked Kalin. The man was moving at a good speed right now, but it couldn't possibly last without stim. Talking would pass the time, whether or not Kalin answered.

"Setting traps," Kalin said, his voice tight with effort.

"Must be a long way off," Pen said.

Kalin didn't answer.

Jocaster could see light from outside. They were only a few meters from the first cavern. He signaled a stop.

"Pen, lead the group out, make contact with Loke before you leave the cavern. We'll hold there until we've tried to reach the ship. Maybe the planet wasn't blocking our signal. Now that we have Kalin, maybe the comms will clear up."

Pen nodded toward Kalin. "You think he was blocking us?"

"I don't know. I'm just going to talk to him before we leave."

"He wouldn't say anything before," Pen said. "What makes you think he'll tell you anything now?"

"I'm not going to ask him about his people," Jocaster said. "I need to know if he's fit enough to come to the shuttles under his own power. If we have to transport him, it's best to know now rather than when we're split up."

Pen glanced between the two men. Jocaster braced for an argument.

"Don't be long," she said. "And don't forget to be careful walking on that debris at the entrance." She turned and hustled the group forward into the cavern.

When they were alone, Jocaster looked Kalin over. He couldn't see any weakness, just the splint as evidence that he must be in agony. "How much pain are you in?"

"Nothing I can't handle." Kalin tried to step around Jocaster.

Jocaster stopped him with a hand to his chest. The man was tough, but he couldn't push Jocaster away; all the will in the world couldn't make up for a damaged body. "Are you going to slow us down?"

"As much as I can, so my soldiers can attack," Kalin said.

"I figured." Jocaster laughed. "I meant, is your injury going to cause problems?"

"I can continue," Kalin said. "The medics on my ship will heal me."

"I'm asking if you can make it back to where you destroyed the shuttles." Jocaster wasn't willing to take a chance that Kalin would be able to report to the ship. They'd pulled off anything that looked like a comm unit to be safe. But the crash site was close enough to their shuttles and if he somehow contacted his ship, it wouldn't be hard to find them.

"If I must," Kalin said.

Jocaster noticed he'd started to list to the left. When he was in motion, Kalin could keep going, but resting was taking its toll.

"Do you have stims?"

"If you mean adrenaline boosters, no. It is not part of our combat kit. We have found it to be more risk than it is worth."

He's getting chatty.

Jocaster didn't have time to take advantage of it, but if he seemed to care, perhaps the man's mood would stay open.

"Before we head out from here, you'll take a dose of ours. I don't want you driving yourself to a standstill."

"When we get out of this mountain, my ship will destroy you on my order."

"Then you won't need the stims," Jocaster said. "Get moving."

KALIN STUMBLED INTO THE LIGHT, blinking to regain his vision. The man, Jocaster, was right to worry about his ability to travel. The pain from his leg sliced through his body with every step. He would soon collapse no matter how much he fought to stay conscious. It was probably already too late for the medics to heal him completely. His days as a combat leader were running out. It did not matter; his commanders would still find use for him. He would not join the workers or the dispossessed on the ship. If he believed that was his fate, he would welcome death at the hands of the Adversary.

"*Dark Prospect* come in." Jocaster was speaking into his open helmet. "There is an enemy ship in orbit."

"Message received, Lieutenant Bryman. Welcome back to the world."

Kalin watched Jocaster take a deep breath, relief if he read the man right. It gave him hope. If the Adversary could reach their ship, then his own would be in range.

"Give me my communication devices," he said. "I will contact my commander."

"Why would I do that?"

"They will know where I am from my tracker." Kalin touched his suit sleeve. "If I don't check in, they will simply destroy everything at my location."

"Including you?"

"I am less important than the survival of my people."

He seemed to consider for a moment. Then just as Kalin marshalled his arguments, Jocaster nodded to the one named Pen to watch him and then walked out of Kalin's hearing.

"Don't be stupid," Pen said. "Tell them you've lost and that they should run."

"What is your rank?"

"I'm a lieutenant. You are a prisoner, which means I outrank you." She handed him the equipment. "Can you talk with your ship while the faceplate is open?"

"Yes, you will hear everything I say. Is there a message you wish to send to mitigate your punishment?"

"Tell them they shouldn't fire on us, or the other ship in orbit," Pen said. "Give us time to talk. We should be allies, not enemies."

"An unlikely concept, but I will not disobey."

He keyed the comm channel. "Kalin reporting."

Kalin kept his eyes focused on Pen. She glared back, clearly not trusting him.

"Kalin to Sola, I have a report." Could he code a message to attack in the communications? Or would being told not to attack by a captured soldier be enough of a message?

No answer.

He checked the helmet power, but it was showing green. "Is your ship blocking my communication?"

"Liz, go ask Jocaster if they are."

The woman returned within moments. "No. They say comms are clear."

Pen squinted at him as though she could read his deepest thoughts.

"Do you think I'm lying? That I have a secret alarm, or code that has initiated battle?"

"Do you?"

"No. We have never had need. But in the future, perhaps it would be a good precaution." Kalin tried one more time to contact Sola. No answer. He saw Jocaster step back into sight. The man was finished with his report, but why did he not tell his people what he had learned?

"Let me try to speak to my soldiers," Kalin said. Perhaps his long-range communications had been damaged when the Adversary had removed them.

Jocaster nodded again.

"Orah, Decai, report." No answer. "Obey me. Report your position."

Nothing. Kalin saw no purpose in trying again — the comms were not working, or he had been left here. "What did your ship tell you?"

"The others know already. I've sent them to wait for instructions farther from the mountain. It's safe for them to be in the open now. Your ship is gone. Your soldiers are gone. They've abandoned you."

Kalin felt hollow. He had never been alone before. Not truly alone. The ship was crowded with people. On this mission he had companions. He was able to speak to Sola. But now, there was no one but these humans he had been taught to hate. "They thought I was killed." Even as he said the words, he knew it was not true. They had not cared. They had left him here with the Adversary.

THEY'D PROPPED him up against a crate. Since there was no apparent threat, the survivors brought out non-essential supplies, perhaps thinking they would ease their entry to the new ship.

Other things had happened in the hour since Kalin felt the weak sun. Families spread out in the open area between the ferns and mountain. Children chased each other around the groupings. He heard laughter. There was community here, and he was alone. Perhaps the Adversary would be merciful and kill him. He didn't have the energy to provoke them, perhaps pity would do as well.

"I guess your people didn't value you as much as you thought," Julie said. She'd been positioned with him, her injured foot raised on a bundle of clothing.

"Survival is the only mission," Kalin said. He saw no point in keeping quiet now. He didn't know where his ship was, so he couldn't put his people in danger.

"You mean their survival, not yours." Julie shifted her weight, wincing as her foot slipped to the ground. "You could teach me how you deal with pain. I had to run on stims. Almost burned me out."

"I doubt you can learn the discipline. You acted on

your own emotions, disobeying direct orders, I imagine." Provocation may work faster with her. And if she was willing to disobey orders, she may kill him. She had a weapon beside her. It was on the ground, and the Adversary felt safe.

"Yep, but I guess my punishment is going to be lighter since I didn't kill you." She nodded toward the groups of civilians. "I have no idea how we're going to support these people."

Kalin didn't answer. He couldn't grasp the concept of disagreeing with superiors. If Julie's commanders wanted to bring more people aboard, it was not her place to deny that. This is why his own people were able to attack so effectively; they followed orders.

Jocaster and Pen approached, carrying food and drink.

"It will be a while longer," Pen said. "*Dark Prospect* is sending shuttles as soon as they are equipped. They'll get ours and bring them here. We should all be aboard in a couple of hours."

"We'll wait in orbit for the other ships to meet us," Jocaster said. "All of them. It will be weeks."

Kalin took the rations and water from Pen. There was no need to resist them any longer. "Why do you tell me your plans?"

"What can you do about them?" Jocaster asked. "Who are you going to tell?"

He didn't need the reminder. "What will your captain do with me?"

"Probably ask you to provide information," Pen said.

"Maybe you'll share a cell in the brig with me," Julie added.

"The captain will decide," Jocaster said. "I know the biggest question. One we all have."

"Ask," Kalin said. He took a bite of the food. It tasted stale and crumbled in his mouth.

"Why were you attacking us? We all came from Earth, right? We are all looking for a home."

"What do you know about why humans left?" Kalin asked.

"The planet was dying," Julie said. "Humans tried, but they couldn't change the future. Asteroids, climate change, the after-effects of war. We had to leave to survive."

"Yes," Kalin said. "That is what we learn also. But we know that it wasn't as unified as you seem to believe. There were factions. Eventually people had to choose between two opposing options. We came to space believing that duty and obedience would save us. In becoming a united community that followed the teachings of our leaders, we believed we would thrive."

"Did it work?" Pen asked.

"No," Kalin said, the word bitter in his mouth. "We broke into smaller factions. Each ship with their own flavor of the true teachings. We fought each other until saner minds rose up. By then only four ships survived to scatter across space. There were occasional reports, at least what our leaders passed on to us. In the end, it seemed that your people, your ships, killed off the others. Now there is only my ship. No, no longer my ship." *Would that pain ever fade?*

"You don't know that we were responsible," Jocaster said. "It's possible, but we were taught that you were the enemy, that you were alien. I guess it started as your philosophy was alien. I don't know that any of our ships survived contact with yours."

"And how many are you?" Kalin asked.

"Like I said, twelve when we went on this mission. Two

ships will join us in a few days. I don't know when the others will come."

Kalin fell silent. He tried to make peace with the idea that these were his people now. The urge to belong was too strong to ignore. Would they accept him eventually, or was his life now counted in days? If their positions were reversed, there would be no mercy for the Adversary. Torture until all information was extracted and then death.

33

Jocaster stood at attention facing the captain. When the shuttles returned to the ship, everyone had been hustled away. Jocaster and his team to the medics for testing and rest. The survivors to modified shuttle bays until they could be assigned homes.

Kalin disappeared with Asher at his side. Julie and Liz had spent one night in the ward. They were gone when Jocaster woke up. Pen still slept as he left to make his report.

"Good work, Lieutenant," the captain said. "You'll see a promotion soon."

"My team deserves recognition," Jocaster said.

"Yes. Your report made that clear. I will be speaking to each of them when they are cleared by the doctors."

"And Kalin?" Jocaster asked, taking advantage of the captain's good mood.

"He is being tended to," the captain said. "Can we trust his information?"

"I think so," Jocaster said. "He took the abandonment hard. As soon as he knew they'd left him, he started talking. I don't think he knows how to live without orders and a community around him. If we treat him right, he'll be a good officer one day. Just needs a little loosening up."

The captain chuckled. "Or my officers need a little tightening up." His face became serious. "I think it would be a mistake to trust him too easily. There are ways to ensure we are getting the truth from someone."

"Torture?" Jocaster wondered where that left them. Probably not on the side of the right.

"Not torture," the Captain said. "We'll do right by him, Lieutenant. Just don't expect to see him in uniform soon."

"Captain?"

"Speak freely, Lieutenant."

"I want to personally commend Lieutenant Tromarin."

"That's not a surprise." The captain looked down at the charts on his desk.

Crap, this was harder than he expected. Pen probably knew it would be. "I know you see us as friends, as a team, maybe. But—"

"Lieutenant, I will give Tromarin her due. I assume your report will be detailed and fair to everyone on the team."

Not the time to argue. Jocaster would do what it took in his report to help Pen.

"May I ask what our next moves are?" Jocaster's curiosity pushed him to the edge of what might be considered acceptable.

"Three more ships have gone out of communication. That leaves us with nine including *Dark Prospect*. Two will be here tomorrow, the others will move in this direction and follow as best they can." The captain turned to look at the star chart displayed on his wall. "Our plans have changed with this new information. We will distribute the survivors between us and go looking for Kalin's ship. We can't afford to let any humans fall away —our lives are too few. Kalin says he can adjust our tracking systems to find traces of the ship. When we have peace, we look for a new home."

Jocaster saluted and left to write his report, already thinking about how to become part of the mission to connect with the enemy ship.

WANT MORE?

Want to join the next thrilling adventure as Pen and Jocaster search for a new home for the remnants of humanity? Use the QR code to grab your copy of FLIGHT.

If you enjoyed reading RESCUE!, please consider helping other readers to find the story by leaving a review.

FREE EBOOK

Claim your copy of Running the Game when you use the QR code below to sign up for my newsletter and cheer on Pen as she vies for a commission in the military.

ALSO BY PA WILSON

For more books by P A Wilson

Use the QR code below or go to pawilson.ca

ABOUT THE AUTHOR

Perry Wilson is a Canadian author based in Vancouver, BC who has big ideas and an itch to tell stories. Having spent some time on university, a career, and life in general, she returned to writing in 2008 and hasn't looked back since (well, maybe a little, but only while parallel parking).

She is a member of the Vancouver Writers Social Group, The Royal City Literary Arts Society, and The Surrey Writing Workshop. Perry has self-published several novels. She writes the Madeline Journeys, a fantasy series about a high-powered lawyer who finds herself trapped in a magical world, the Quinn Larson Quests, which follows the adventures of a wizard named Quinn who must contend with volatile fae in the heart of Vancouver, and the Charity Deacon Investigations, a mystery thriller series about a private eye who tends to fall into serious trouble with her cases, and The Riverton Romances, a series based in a small town in Oregon, one of her favorite states. Her stand-alone novels are Breaking the Bonds, Closing the Circle, and The Dragon at The Edge of The Map.

For more information
www.pawilson.ca
pawilson@pawilson.ca

ACKNOWLEDGMENTS

People think that the process of writing is solitary. That's not the case for me. I have help from so many people it would be hard to acknowledge everyone, but I'll give it a try.

The support and inspiration I get from my writer's groups is incalculable. The Vancouver Writers Social Group opens my mind to other ways of telling a story. The Royal City Literary Arts Society gives me the opportunity to meet and share with other writers who have more knowledge than I do. The Other 11 Months group is where I learn about getting the words on the page. And my critique group who helps me find the best parts of the story I want to tell. Thanks to all of the members of these great groups.

Last of all, but definitely a huge part of the process, my beta readers. These are the people who love stories and are willing, and more than able, to tell me if my finished story is ready for you, my readers.